The Cat Burglar

by

Wm. Dudley

Dedication

For Tyler and Storm

Contents

The Cat Burglar:
The Tempest

One

In the darkening shadows of a dim evening a small, tawny brown cat slowly edged his way down a cluttered alley. At thirteen months old and barely eight pounds, he was considered small when compared with other cats. He wanted to be big, even dreamed of it when he slept, but his parents had not been large and he did not hold out much hope for his own growth. He tried to talk big and act big, but in reality he was just a quiet and rather mild cat. He preferred the companionship of his friends and snuggling with his humans in the evenings, to rough and tumble play.

He looked slowly around the alley, at the garbage bins, rusted cars and dilapidated cardboard boxes. He felt out of place here. His humans lived in a large apartment in a wealthy gated community on the far south side of town. He had good food, a warm bed to sleep on and plenty of attention when he wanted it. Being in this part of town, amongst the seediest of cats was far beyond his realm of comfort. As much as he didn't want to admit it, he was scared.

He tried to calm his nerves by remembering that he was attempting to help his humans, but try as he might he couldn't shake the feeling that he could be making a giant mistake. He had left his comfortable home, traveled to the darkest side of town, seeking an enigmatic character who probably didn't even really exist. What a fool I am, he thought, I'll probably not make it out of here alive.

He was looking for a cat known only as The Cat Burglar. And if that is not a mysterious name, he said to himself, nothing is. The Cat Burglar was more than renowned, he was a legend. No one was even sure he was real, he may be nothing more than a myth. But, if he is real, the small cat thought, he is the only one who can help.

He had first heard of The Cat Burglar a couple months ago. It was a story a neighbor kitten had told him to scare him when he was little. Not that he was big or old now, but he had been even smaller then. The Cat Burglar was a horror story kittens were told either to make them behave for their parents, as in "You better behave or The Cat Burglar will get you", or something other kittens told you to see how tough you were. He had never felt very tough.

But for all that, he knew that if anyone could help him it would be this phantom, this unreal specter known as The Cat Burglar. So here he was, sloshing through the muck and slime of a grimy, wet alley, trying to maintain his concentration and his outward show of strength.

While looking down to step over a pile of litter and skirt a rancid puddle he failed to notice that he was suddenly surrounded by a large and very angry looking mob of ragtag alley cats. With a shudder he came to an abrupt stop. "Who… umm… who are you?" he asked with the fear making his voice quiver.

"Who are we?" asked the largest and meanest looking of the cats, a dusty black giant with a scar running from one eye to the other and a portion of his ear missing, "I must say, you have a lot of guts asking questions of us. After all, you are the pampered little squat of a kitten who has come into our alley. It is not we who came to your home for a cup of milk and a chat." at this the gang started laughing hysterically, repeating portions of his comments.

"Little squat of a kitten." one howled.

"A cup of milk and a chat." another chortled, as the whole group rolled with laughter.

"I… uh… I am called Jaffa" the little cat said softly, "I… I've come to talk to The Cat Burglar."

At this, all sound in the alley stopped. The cats immediately resumed their upright positions and stared at the little kitten. Gone was the laughing, and Jaffa was certain he could sense fear in the air.

"What do you want with The Cat Burglar?" the large black cat said with a growl.

"So he is real, huh?" Jaffa said quickly.

"Again with the questions. This is our alley… we ask, you answer." the giant hissed.

"I… I'm sorry… I… I have a bit of a problem and I think only The Cat Burglar can help." Jaffa said in a rush. He was on uncomfortable ground here, he had no idea who he could trust and who he couldn't, he only knew he needed to try talking to The Cat Burglar.

Just then, a large cat moved out of the shadows. He was an amazingly beautiful animal. Not as well groomed as Jaffa, and he obviously did not live in a nice house with caring humans, but still a remarkably well kept animal. His coat was the shade of grey one sees from an oil fire. Deep, charcoal grey with a hint of brightness when the light hit it. His chest and belly were a pale beige and his eyes were the brightest shade of green Jaffa had ever seen. This, Jaffa thought, was not a cat to be on the bad side of.

As the large grey cat moved forward, Jaffa found himself moving slowly backward. He had made a giant mistake and it was now time to leave. "I... I really should be... you know... going now. I... umm... I'm sorry to have interrupted your evening." with that he started to turn and leave, when he heard the big grey cat say in a deep voice, "Stop." Jaffa turned slowly and looked into those brilliant green eyes, "You said you had something to discuss with The Cat Burglar, what is it?"

Jaffa looked around at the gathered mob, "Umm... yeah, well... I was kind of hoping to talk to him in private you see." he stammered.

"Leave." the large grey cat said and Jaffa began to turn, "Not you, little one, them." Jaffa turned to see all the other cats running off quickly down the alley, "Now, what did you have to discuss with The Cat Burglar?"

"Well... Sir... it's rather a delicate issue, and I... well, if The Cat Burglar were around, I would like to... you know... ummm... well, talk to him." Jaffa said.

"Jaffa... relax... I am The Cat Burglar." he said with a chuckle, "Come along with me." as the Cat Burglar turned and strolled down the alley, Jaffa breathed a sigh of relief and followed.

* * *

At the end of the alley was a dark entryway. A quick calculation told Jaffa that the entry was roughly ten feet square and twelve feet high. The entry was brick and had an arched top. The building it belonged to was one of the oldest in town. In its lifetime, it had been a hotel, a hospital, an office building and an apartment building. Now it was deserted. Most of the doors would not open and most of the windows would not close. No animals, other than rats, would enter for fear of contracting some unnamed disease, or having the dilapidated old building fall down on them.

But here in the doorway, nestled into the corner, was an old leather chair. It was a bit worse for wear, but not as bad as one would expect considering it was exposed to the elements year round. Much of the brown stain had worn off, and white padding showed through in places, but for all that it appeared warm and comfortable. It was there that The Cat Burglar jumped up to, and lay down to rest. Jaffa, for his part, sat quietly in front of the big chair and felt the tension begin to seep out of his muscles.

"Thank you for taking time to see me, Sir, I know you must be very busy. I... I really wasn't sure you were real. I thought I might be wasting my time... and placing myself in a lot of danger at the same time." Jaffa stammered. He was rushing his words in his nervousness and was finding it hard to relax.

"I must say," The Cat Burglar said in his deep rumble of a voice, "I am always amazed that the other animals do not think I am real. It's not like I hide out and keep a low profile, you know. I've been hanging out in or around this alley for over five years. I have no idea how this whole mystique began." The Cat Burglar chuckled.

"Well, it's a very strange world we live in, Sir." Jaffa said softly.

The Cat Burglar burst out laughing at this, "My, how right you are little one. You have no idea some of the strange things I have seen." he said as his eyes crinkled up in laughter, "So tell me, Jaffa, what brings you from The Heights, all the way up here to our part of the city?"

"How... ummm... how did you know I am from The Heights?" Jaffa asked with a perplexed look on his face.

"Well, it's really not that hard to figure out, little one. You speak clearly and properly, definitely not alley speak. Your coat is beautifully cared for, you appear well fed and exercised, if a bit soft around the middle, and you are wearing a leather collar, with a name tag and address on it. We cats can't read human, of course, so I don't know what the tags say, but otherwise, honestly, it would be hard for me to not know where you were from."

"Well, I could be from another part of town, like Jones, or The Willows." Jaffa countered.

"Cats from Jones are more working class cats. They are well trimmed, but have a bit of a rough edge, which you don't. And Cats from The Willows are pampered and lazy, also something you are not." The Cat Burglar smiled, he was having fun with this little one.

"Oh… I see." Jaffa was starting to feel a bit overwhelmed. The Cat Burglar was much older, wiser and more street savvy than he was, he felt out of place here. He decided to get to the point.

"Well you see, Sir… over where I live… you know… The Heights… umm… well, there have been some things going on which I think we need some help with." Jaffa stammered. Now that he was here and ready to explain, he felt foolish. Surely he was wasting his time.

"Go on." The Cat Burglar said, as he leaned forward in his chair to concentrate more closely.

"Well, sir… you see, some things are… well… missing from the building I live in." Jaffa said quickly.

"And you thought since my name has the word Burglar in it, I might be involved?" The Cat Burglar said with a hint of laughter in his voice. This was fun, he thought.

"WHAT??? NO!! OF COURSE NOT!" Jaffa screeched as he jumped up and back from where he was sitting, "I wasn't thinking anything of the sort, really I wasn't." Jaffa said as fast as he could, fear making his voice rise. He could feel himself start to shiver.

"Relax, Jaffa, I'm only joking. My, you are a nervous little one, aren't you? O.K., let's start over. Items are missing from your building and you came to me. If these are human things, why come to me, it's for the humans to figure out." The Cat Burglar was confused. Why would cats get involved in the affairs of humans?

"Well, yes, Sir, they are the property of the humans, but I am pretty sure it is not humans who took the items." Jaffa said softly, he felt he could be making a fool of himself here.

"Why not?" The Cat Burglar asked.

"Well, the humans have had their police in, and talked to all the neighbors and no one has seen anything. "

"How many apartments are we talking about here?"

"Four, so far, Sir" Jaffa began to relax, maybe The Cat Burglar was going to help, he thought.

"Is there anything the apartments all have in common?"

"Well, Sir, all of those apartments are on the third floor, and all of them are facing the same side of the building."

"I see, and have all the robberies been recent?"

"Yes, Sir. All in the past two weeks."

"Jaffa, I need you to take me there and show me. Can you do that?"

"Yes, Sir, I can."

"Great, let's get going. Oh, and Jaffa." The Cat Burglar said softly.

"Yes, Sir?"

"Most of the animals just call me CB."

"Oh, thank you, Sir… I mean CB. To be honest, 'Sir' seemed awful formal, and 'The Cat Burglar' is really quite a mouthful,"

The two cats laughed as they began their stroll out of the alley.

Two

The Heights was the area on the far south side of town. The humans living there were wealthy by human terms, but not outrageously so. They still had to work for a living, it's just that their work required more thought than muscle.

Many of the homes in this area were large with sprawling lawns. But most of the humans had chosen to live in large apartment buildings or condominium buildings, within gated communities. A safety thing it was assumed. The building Jaffa lived in was one of the larger ones. Seven stories high and a block long, it was a marvel of beautiful cream-colored brick. At each floor, just below the windows, was a fieldstone ledge running around the entire building.

As Jaffa pointed out the four apartments which had been broken into, CB began making mental notes. Each apartment had an open window, with no covering screen. Each window was within inches of the ledge running around the building, and each apartment was on the third floor. Not far from where they were standing was a large oak tree, whose branches hung to within eight feet of the building and slightly above the ledge on the third floor.

"It's a cat." CB said almost to himself.

"What?" Jaffa asked as if he hadn't heard.

"It's a cat that is breaking in and taking things."

"How do you know?" Jaffa asked in astonishment.

"He's using the tree to climb up and get out on those branches which are close to the ledge. An eight foot jump is nothing to a cat, and the fact that the branches are slightly above the ledge is an even bigger asset." CB said, settling into his role as a teacher.

"Why would the height of the branch matter?"Jaffa asked, perplexed.

CB smiled. He loved this. Figuring out the way in was always his favorite part of the game, "A cats natural jump is in an arc. Up, over and back down. A situation like this one, being slightly higher, allows the cats natural arc to carry him further. In other words he can cover more distance, with less effort."

"Oh, I see."

"Have any of the apartments had animals in them of any sort?" CB asked.

"Ummm… no, not that I can think of. Why would that matter?" Jaffa was feeling well out of his league here.

"Definitely a cat. As you know we cats have a very well developed sense of smell. We know almost immediately if there is another animal around. If there is, they will make noise if a cat were to enter the house. When stealing from a house, you don't want noise. Also, notice the open windows."

"What about the windows? Lots of places have their windows open this time of year, the weather is beautiful."

"Yes, but these windows don't have screens. Humans won't leave a window open without a screen if they have an animal in the house. They are too afraid the animal will leap out the window."

"Oh, I see. But why are you so sure it's a cat?"

"Well, a dog isn't going to climb the tree to be able to get to the third floor. A bird could get there, but wouldn't be able to carry off much at one time, they don't have the strength. Obviously things like rats, mice, gerbils and such are out of the question. No… he's a cat, and a young one I would guess. Maybe a bit older than you, perhaps a year and a half old."

"O.k… go ahead and explain that to me. How in the world can you tell his age? By the way, how do you know it's a male cat?"

"Oh, I'm not really a hundred percent certain it's a male, but female burglars are unusual in the cat community. It could be female, but not likely. As for the age, it has to do with the mode of entry. You see, when burglars start out they find the simplest ways to get in to wherever they are trying to rob. As they get older, they take more risks and look for bigger challenges. This mode of entry is fairly sophisticated, but not the biggest challenge in the world. He's young, but not new to the game. He's also very smart and very confident. I think I'm going to like this guy."

"I don't understand, what makes you think you will like him?"

"Oh, that's easy, he reminds me of myself when I was young."

"You mean you used to do this sort of thing when you were that young?"

"Well, no, not that young, my life of crime didn't start until I was a bit older. But, yes, this is what I used to do for a living. Where do you think my name came from?"

"Oh, yeah… sorry, I forgot about your name. What made you stop doing that?"

"What makes you think I stopped. My name isn't 'Former Cat Burglar'."

"Yeah, well... umm... I see. But I had the impression you spent your time helping now, rather than stealing. I'm sorry if I jumped to the wrong conclusion." Jaffa was getting confused, this was not at all what he expected.

"Don't worry, little one, I'm out of the game now. But helping others requires a lot of the same skills that I needed when I was younger. I just apply them a little differently."

"O.k... let me see if I have this all correct. We are looking for a cat. He is using the tree to climb up to the higher level branches and jump over to the third floor. He then walks along the ledge to apartments with open windows and sniffs to see if there is another animal inside. If so, he moves on to the next open window, if not, he goes in, finds what he wants, takes it and leaves. Right?"

"Yep, you are correct."

'But why is he only taking small things like rings, watches, bracelets, necklaces and so on?"

"Jaffa, you were doing so well. Think it through, why wouldn't he take bigger things?"

"Oh, yeah... it would be too big to carry out with him, jump back to the tree and get back down to the ground. Sorry."

"Don't apologize, you are new to this game, I am not. I need to be able to work these things through quickly, you don't. So, yes, you are right all across the board. Thanks for bringing this to my attention."

"So, do you know who this cat is?"

"I don't think so. I know all the older cats and keep a close eye on their activity. I even know most of the younger cats. But this one has a new signature. This is really pretty clever. This isn't the most complicated process, but it isn't simple either. I'm pretty sure this is a cat I don't know. I look forward to meeting him."

"So, what do we do now?"

"Well, you get to go home, curl up on your comfortable couch and snuggle up with your humans. I hope they're good to you."

"Oh, yes, they are great. They're kind and caring, I like them immensely, they're good people."

"Most of them are. So, you go home to them and be happy. Me, well, I get to go to work. I need to meet this little punk and see what's in his head. I'll keep you up to date as things go along, but one way or another I'll put an end to this and see if I can get any of the missing things back."

"O.K. Ummm… CB… is it polite of me to say, take care of yourself?"

"Absolutely, in fact, I appreciate it. Now get home and get some rest. You have done an important thing today. Let's hope for a quick and safe end to this game."

With a quick butting of heads, the two new friends said goodbye and Jaffa ran off to his home. With a chuckle, CB strolled into a copse of bushes on the far side of the oak tree. The burglar wouldn't arrive until later at night. CB had plenty of time for a rest before the game began. With a yawn and stretch of his muscles, he lay down in the dark underbrush and took a nap.

Three

It took three nights before CB finally heard the new cat coming into the yard by the oak tree. It was a dark and warm night and his comfort had left him well rested and alert. It was only this that had allowed him to hear the other cat. Had he been sleepy or less rested, the other cats silent approach would have gone unnoticed. As the cat stepped out of the bushes and into the moonlit evening, CB got his first look at the newest burglar in town.

As CB had anticipated, it was a young cat, but even in this light he could see a hint of depth and wisdom in this new cat. He stood approximately the same height and was the same length as CB, and had a tail as long as his body. His sense of balance had to be incredible with that tail as a counter-balance. Weight-wise he still had a young cat look to him, lithe and lanky, and just starting to fill in the muscle around the shoulders and haunches.

His coat was blacker than midnight in a thunderstorm with a pale grey around the front of his neck and running down his chest. All of this made him a handsome animal, but what really caught CB's attention and truly stood out for him was the tip of the young cats fur. Along both of his sides and down the sides of his tail the jet black fur was tipped in white. Yet, there was a stripe of deepest black running from between the young cats ears, across his head and back and all the way to the tip of his tail.

CB found the markings fascinating. They gave the little cat the look of a black cat who had been caught in a snowstorm. Looking down on him from above, in shadows, he would blend in with the dark ground around him and not be noticeable until he moved. The same thing would happen looking up at him from the ground, with his lighter markings and frosted fur, he would blend in with the lighter sky and not be easily seen. He was an almost flawless burglar… he was essentially invisible.

All of this CB noticed in a fraction of a second, but what surprised him was something he had not anticipated. He saw, in complete astonishment, that the new cat was wearing a black collar around his light grey throat.

In that split second, the small cat had time to notice CB and immediately turned to face him, puffing up his tail and hunching his back at the same time. A low hiss emanated from the young animal.

"No sense puffing up to look bigger, I have already seen you and know how big you are." CB said calmly, still curled in his hunched, seated position.

"Well… since I don't know you, or what you want, I think I'll just remain prepared, if you don't mind." the new cat said with a low growl.

"Oh, by all means, suit yourself. Whatever makes you happy." CB said nonchalantly.

"What would make me happy is for you to leave and let me carry on with my business." came the response.

"Well… I am pretty sure we both know that isn't going to happen. So tell me, what is this business of yours?"

"Nothing of concern to you, I am certain. Just here for a little stroll and stretch of my legs."

"Ah, I see. And would that stretching of your legs include climbing an oak tree, walking to the end of a branch, jumping onto a ledge, finding an open window of an apartment that doesn't have an animal in the house, climbing in the unscreened window and making off with bright and shiny things that don't belong to you?"

The young cat stared at CB for several seconds before responding, "Hmmmm…" he said finally, "what I can't figure out is whether you are here to stop me from doing just what you described, or if you have figured out the same plan and are working on the execution of it even as we speak."

"Oh, no worries, little one, I am well out of the business you are in. I'm not here to steal your plan, or anything else for that matter. Unfortunately, I can't allow you to steal anything else, either. It's this thing I do, you know. Stopping cats like you from doing silly things."

"Wait… I know you, you're The Cat Burglar, aren't you?" the little cat said with a touch of awe and wonder in his voice, "I didn't think you really existed."

"Yeah, I get that a lot." CB said with frustrated sarcasm in his voice, "But yes, I really do exist. You can call me CB, it's a lot easier than saying the whole thing. And what am I to call you"

"Yes, CB is easier to say. I'll keep that in mind if we cross paths again. Technically, my name is Storm, but most of the time I'm referred to as 'The Storm'."

"Oh, Brother!!! You have GOT to be kidding me!!!" CB said with dripping exasperation.

"Hey, The Storm is, who The Storm is. If you can't handle the strain, just move outside the range of the blizzard."

"Oh, great, you also talk about yourself in the third person. As if using the word 'The' in front of your name wasn't annoying enough. Alright… The Storm… let's move this along so we can both get back to a more realistic world."

"Oh, you have the nerve to talk about my name… you, who has chosen a name for himself which isn't technically a name at all… it's more of a title, isn't it."

"Fair enough, I'll give you that one, but at least there isn't a blizzard following me that other animals need to move out of range of."

"That's enough of the sarcasm, how about showing a little respect."

At this, CB shot up into a standing position and leaned toward the smaller cat, "Respect is earned, Storm, not a birthright." CB said with anger in his voice, "Show me some behaviors and attitudes that deserve some respect and I'll show the respect that is due."

"Big words for a fat, old cat like you. How about putting your paws and teeth where your words are. This is my territory, not yours."

"A favor was asked of me. This is now my territory."

"So be it." Storm said, and with lightening reflexes he launched himself at CB. The motion was so fast it was almost impossible to see. In microseconds the battle was on.

Storm launched himself at CB's left flank, with his front paws spread wide, all claws extended and his fangs bared for the attack. But, when he reached the spot where CB had been standing he found nothing. CB was gone, and he felt a sharp smack on the back of his head that made him see stars for a second.

"That was an interesting move, Storm. I have always liked it. But there's a trick to it if you want to use it correctly. You need to have the front of your body going to the right, but your hips going to the left. That way you cut off your opponents escape." CB said as if he was teaching a pupil.

He had no more finished speaking than Storm launched his second attack, a feint to the right, followed by a quick leap and twist. This time he felt his right forepaw catch the tip of CB's ear. But when he landed and turned again to see where his foe was, all he felt was a sharp smack on the back of his head and saw more stars.

"A much better move, I must say. I'll give you a hint of respect for that move. It was actually fairly unique. If you had a bit more muscle mass that might have been quite a challenging move to escape. Unfortunately, strength and experience are in my favor. Do keep that one in your playbook though, it will be a handy move in the future."

As CB's last word came out Storm launched his next attack, head on, and directly at CB's chest. The older cat dodged this with ease, but in mid air Storm changed direction and was full at CB's back, CB barely avoided the second attack and as soon as Storm's feet touched the ground, he spun again and this time hit CB squarely on his right shoulder. CB staggered for a second before shifting his hips to the left and knocking Storm's feet out from under him. As Storm rolled to his back, CB landed on his chest, settled all his weight on Storm's belly and sank his teeth into Storms throat. The battle was over.

"Werry neish moo, Shtor." CB said with a mouth full of fur.

"What?" Storm choked, feeling CB's fangs constricting his breathing.

"I shed, werry neish… oh, da heck wish it, ish har to alk ish ay." CB slurred.

"Then let me go."

"No ay! Ish leshon ty."

With this, Storm let loose with a violent struggle, but he was no match for CB's strength and weight. After a few seconds he settled back down. This time however, CB's teeth were even tighter in his throat.

"Let go of me." he gasped.

"Nau util oo ar eddy oo issen."

"This is stupid, we can't understand each other. I promise not to fight if you let go of my throat." Storm said in a whisper, the last of his breath being squeezed out of him.

"Ine, ut ish oo fite, I ill gab oor troat agen."

"Whatever… let me go."

At this CB loosened his grip and sat back. With all of CBs weight on him, Storm could not move.

"Yuck, I hate having fur in my mouth. If you fight again, I will grab your throat again. And by the way, it isn't a collar I saw, is it? It's a black stripe in your fur. That's really great, it will fool almost any animal or human into thinking you are tame. What a great asset. Anyway, what I said was, that was a very nice move, I am very impressed. Where did you learn that?"

"Thanks for the complement. I made that move up a while ago, when I had to get away from this giant Akita who works as a guard dog for my human. She's not very pleasant and doesn't seem to like cats."

"Wait, are you talking about Kieko? A giant long haired female, mostly black and white, with a huge black head surrounded by a big grey mane?"

"Yeah, do you know her?"

"Sure, everyone knows her. The humans hire her out to whoever pays the most. She is really not very pleasant. She's also fairly bright for a dog, and you know how dangerous a combination size, strength and intelligence can be."

"So now what, CB, do I get to listen to a lecture or do you just let me go?" Storm asked with growing boredom.

"No, no lectures, you are far too young to waste my breath on lectures. We are just going to come to an agreement. I will let you up. In return, you will show me where your human lives, and you will stop stealing from these people."

"And if I refuse?"

"Well, I have fairly strong jaws, I'll make it quick."

"Oh, give me a break, you wouldn't kill me."

"You are much too young to make a mistake that big when judging other animals, Storm. We are animals, we do what we must to survive."

Storm stared into CB's deep green eyes for a second and thought about fighting further, but in those eyes he saw a firm commitment. With a sigh, he allowed his muscles to relax. He was beaten.

"Fine, I agree to the terms. I will leave these buildings alone, though they were very easy pickings. But, I can't tell you where my human lives."

In a flash, CB spun his head to the right, lowered it and had Storm's throat in his mouth again. This time Storm felt real danger. He could barely breath and his eyes were losing focus. This time, CB was serious.

"O.K., O.K…. stop." Storm gasped, he couldn't take much more of this he was rapidly losing consciousness, his body already beginning to spasm from strain.

Again, CB let loose of Storm's throat, "I am not joking around here, Storm. This is not a game of maybe and perhaps. You will tell me what I need to know and live, or play around and die, it's your choice."

"O.K., fine. Geez, lighten up. My human and I recently moved to a small shack on Deeter Street near the canal, actually not far from the alley that rumor says you live in. But, if my human finds out I told you, he'll be furious."

"Yeah, you really don't have to worry about that now do you, Storm. Remember, humans can't understand animals."

"Oh, yeah, I forgot about that."

"Alright, I am going to let you up now, but before I do, it's time for that lecture we talked about earlier. I still think you are too young for it, but I'm a sucker for it. You are obviously a very smart cat. You are also street wise, agile, and fast. You are wasting your skills stealing shiny baubles from humans, even if you are getting some form of treat from your human. We need cats with your skills working for us, not against us. Now, knowing you will ignore what I just said, I'm going to let you get up, but just remember I will be watching you."

"Thanks for the warning, Dad. See you soon." with this Storm started to rise, but CB adjusted his weight and held Storm in place for a few more seconds.

"No, Storm, I'm not your Dad. Though I wish I were, you are far too talented to go to waste. Just think about this question, Storm. Does your human have you around because he cares about you, or because you are talented in stealing shiny objects? Think about that carefully, though I am not sure you will like the answer." with that parting shot, he jumped off Storm and stood back waiting to see if there would be another attack from the young upstart.

"My human cares a lot about me, CB. Too bad you never had a human who cared about you." Storm said as he started to run off.

"Oh, how wrong you are." CB whispered, and turned toward Deeter Street.

Four

"Nothing?? You returned with nothing. How dare you? What were you thinking?" Storm's human screamed when Storm returned. As Storm ran to hide under the couch, a shoe bounced above his head. He had seen his human angry before, that was part of living with humans. But this was something more. His human was almost out of control. He knew his human cared about him… of course he did… but this is what he could expect when he failed in his job. This was all CB's fault.

When his human finally seemed to calm down, Storm crawled out from under the couch and approached his human cautiously. With a rub against his humans leg, he felt a rough hand close rapidly around his neck and he was suddenly lifted off the ground and found himself staring into his humans angry eyes.

"Never… never … fail me again." his human yelled, while Storm shrank away in fear. Then, his human set him down and ran his rough hand across the fur of his head, "Now, let me get you some food and you can head out again tomorrow morning." see, Storm thought, he really does care.

* * *

CB sat quietly listening to the rantings of Storm's human and felt his heart go out to the small cat. If a human really cares for you, this kind of yelling does not occur. Sure, they may yell from time to time when you are doing something dangerous, or destructive, but once you learn their rules, the yelling ends. Storm needed to learn that this human was not right for him.

As CB turned and started to move away from the house, a giant black and white Akita came racing up to him yelling at the top of her voice, "Get away from here, how dare you show your head around here? Just wait until I get my teeth on you, you worthless bag of fur."

CB stopped where he was and turned slowly to look at the giant dog, "Ah… Kieko… it's been a while. How is life in the drooling and chewing world?"

With this, Kieko let loose a torrent of angry and wholly incomprehensible gibberish, "That sounds a lot like just noise, Kieko. How about you calm down and we have a bit of a chat."

"After you die, we can talk, CB." Kieko yelled.

"Ummm… exactly how would that work? I doubt very much I will be able to talk much after I die." CB chuckled.

At this, Kieko stopped screaming and stared at CB, "What?" she said finally.

"I said, it's not likely that we can talk after I die, so let's talk now." CB said with a smile.

"Talk about what, fur bag?" Kieko growled.

"Oh… really… do we have to be so specific. We are old… well… friends, may not be the correct word, but at least we can admit to being old acquaintances. We haven't seen each other for a while. Let's start there. Last time I saw you, you were working for that old woman over by the river who was stealing other humans plants, wasn't it?" CB laughed.

At this Kieko laughed in turn, "That woman was crazy beyond words." Kieko smiled, "I never could figure out what the heck she was trying to do. Remember she had hundreds of plants stuffed in her garage. I could see if she was going to plant them, but all she did was stuff them in the garage, close the door and let them die off."

CB let out a howl of laughter at this memory, "I remember that, she really was quite insane, wasn't she? I never really felt like I accomplished much by shutting her activities down. She wasn't really hurting anyone, just more annoying and costing them."

"Yeah," Kieko said, "but you still ended up losing my job for me. How am I supposed to be a guard dog, if I don't have anything to guard?"

"Well, I guess that's a good question. Is that what you are doing here, guarding something?" CB asked.

"Now... CB... you know I can't answer that." Kieko said with her hackles starting to rise, "What are you planning, CB?"

"Who, me... planning something... I can't imagine." CB said, "Of course, you know I can't allow your human to keep using Storm the way he is. It's not only wrong for the human, but it's fairly demeaning to the cat."

"Demeaning to the cat... is there such a thing?" Kieko chuckled, "You know I can't allow you to interfere here, and if you stop Storm from returning without some loot again, our human will likely kick him out... or kill him. Storm is too stupid to realize his situation"

"No, Kieko, Storm isn't stupid... not by a long way. What he is, is in search of some attention. And negative attention is still attention. I really think he is a pretty good kid, he just needs some guidance." CB said.

25

"Ah, CB… always the optimist. You better try and get to him soon, his role here won't last long if he isn't allowed to do his job. Of course, you'll need to get through me first." Kieko growled.

"We'll see, Kieko… we'll see." CB said and started to walk away, "Tell me, Kieko, have you chosen who your next human will be?"

"And what, may I ask CB, makes you think I will be in need of another human in the near future?" Kieko said with a hesitant chuckle.

"Well, Kieko, we've been here before, haven't we? You know what your human is doing. I know what your human is doing. And we both know that there is no way I am going to allow it to continue. Therefore, you are soon to be in need of a new human. The questions are, who is it going to be, and what am I going to have to do to stop them from doing whatever it is they are doing? Because I assure you, whoever your next human is, they will be every bit as crooked as the last two." Kieko stared at CB with fury in her eyes. The arrogance of this fat grey cat knew no bounds.

"I warn you, CB, never get close enough to let my claws or teeth do the work they are hired to do." with this, Kieko turned and started walking away, "Stay away from here CB. That's a warning."

"Warning taken, Kieko. But know one thing. In that house is a small cat, who is still barely more than a kitten. He is being used and taken advantage of, just like you, by one of the worst types of humans. And while he may be a cocky little kitten, there is a goodness in him waiting to come out. I will not let him be hurt. By you, or by the human in that house." and with that, CB turned his back to Kieko and walked off down the street.

Two houses down, and well out of the sight of Kieko, CB turned and headed back to the house on Deeter Street and watched from the bushes. Storm would be safe for tonight, he was certain. But tomorrow, he would again be stopped from doing his human's bidding by CB. Two days without bringing back trinkets for his human would put Storm in grave danger. Tomorrow would need to be a very important day.

Five

Storm left the house on Deeter Street the next morning just as the sun was cresting the horizon. He stayed in the shadows, using the deep greys to work together with his own natural camouflage and make him largely invisible. He knew he couldn't return to the apartments he had been going to for the past few weeks, CB would be keeping an eye on them to make sure he didn't return. No matter though, he thought, he had other places he could go to.

He walked in the shadows for four blocks then turned north and headed toward The Willows. As the wealthiest part of town, the humans there not only had plenty of shiny toys that his human would love, but they were also pampered enough to believe they were safe from theft. Storm chuckled. Ahh, humans, they can be so naïve.

The Willows had a fence surrounding it, and a giant gated entrance. Any human trying to gain entrance would have trouble getting in. A cat, especially a thin one, would have no problem whatsoever fitting between the wrought iron railings of the gate. He could slip in and out unnoticed.

On the south side of the fence, near a wooded area, Storm slipped between two iron railings and headed toward the first house he saw.

"Well… I guess that's about as far as I can really allow you to go. This was a pretty clever idea, though. Of course it was pretty easy to figure out, and following you is not the hardest thing I have ever had to do. You could use a few lessons in being stealthy, but we'll get to that." CB said calmly from beneath a small bush not five feet from Storm.

Storm jumped three feet in the air and let out a low howl at the shock of hearing CB's voice. His tail puffed out to its largest as he laid his ears back and assumed a fighting posture.

"What are you doing here? Leave me be, I have work to do." Storm hissed.

"Work? Is that what you call it? It looks more like stealing to me. You know what they say about stealing, don't you? No? Well, it's pretty simple... if it doesn't belong to you... leave it alone!" CB said, emphasizing the last three words.

"Why don't you leave me alone, old man. I have really lost patience with you. You got lucky in yesterday's fight, you won't be so fortunate this time." with this, Storm launched himself at CB, feinting to the right, then twisting left at the last second. When he arrived where CB was, he once again found his prey missing and felt a smack against the back of his head.

"Isn't this where we left off yesterday?" CB said with a laugh, "No, wait, yesterday we ended up with a hunk of your neck fur in my mouth. Do you really want to try this again?"

Storm responded with a hiss and another attack. Taking a head-on approach, he ran straight at CB, then, just at the last second, as CB was beginning to move, Storm stopped and reversed his direction while jumping four feet in the air and lashing out with his hind legs. CB almost got caught when he started laughing halfway through this movement. Storm landed almost a foot away without ever getting close to CB.

"What in the world was that?" CB laughed.

"A change of mind." Storm said, then with lightening speed he reversed direction again and caught CB off guard and laughing. Storm's right paw caught CB on the very edge of his chin, his razor sharp claws drawing a small bead of blood from CB.

"Very good, Storm." CB said, no longer laughing. "That was very good, you caught me off guard, sorry, I have a healthy sense of humor, it distracts me. I don't recommend you expect that to happen again."

"You haven't seen anything yet, old man." the speed of his next attack was almost too fast for CB to see. This kitten had amazing talent, he thought again. Good thing he's so young and inexperienced. As Storm's attack came at him from what seemed to be four different directions, CB leaned as far back on his haunches as he could without losing his balance and just as Storm reached his closest point, CB shot forward as fast as he could in a massive head-butt. As his forehead smacked into the side of Storm's head he heard a crunch like nothing he had heard in years. Storm crumbled under the weight of the crushing blow and collapsed in a lifeless form.

CB shook his head to clear the cobwebs that formed from the blow. He needed to remember not to do that move again in the near future, he had almost knocked himself out in the process. As his eyes cleared he walked over to Storm's inert body, laid his ear against Storm's chest to make sure he wasn't actually dead, and was comforted by the sound of slow breathing and a shallow heartbeat. Good, he thought, he's still alive.

Reaching over with his teeth, he grabbed Storm by the scruff of his neck and pulled him under one of the nearest bushes. Taking a deep breath he sat back and waited for Storm to wake up. When fifteen minutes passed he began to get concerned that he may have done more damage than he expected, but at twenty minutes, Storm's hind legs began a slow twitch and his eye fluttered open.

"Thank goodness, little one, I was afraid I had killed you." CB said softly, true concern obvious in his voice.

"What the heck was that? What did you hit me with?" Storm's voice sounded distant and groggy, it would be a few minutes before he truly came around.

"I hit you with my head." CB said softly. Storm would undoubtedly have a headache, better not to talk too loud, "It's called a headbutt. If done correctly, it hurts your opponent much more than it hurts yourself. Though, to be honest, I am still not sure I am seeing correctly yet. The down side is that if you hit your opponent wrong, you can kill them."

"I thought a headbutt was something we cats did to show affection." Storm said quietly.

"It is, if we have a good human, or want to acknowledge a friend, or a special little female cat, you want to show your affection to. But, as with most things it has two sides. I was concerned using that technique on you, my little friend, you are far too important and special for me to kill you."

"I do have a good human. He loves me. But what do you mean important and special? What are you talking about?" Storm said as he began to work the kinks out of his muscles. The fight was out of him.

"Storm, you are incredibly smart, amazingly talented and have the makings of a fantastic fighter. All of those are traits I have need of. But, I need you to listen to me." CB said as earnestly as he possibly could.

"Why would you need me to listen to you? I'm just a young upstart, obviously I haven't come into full use of my 'amazing talents'."

"Because, Storm, you do not have a good human. Sure, he has a great cat, but you don't have a good human. There are a lot of different humans out there. Most humans are fabulous. They are kind and caring and truly love having us around them as companions. But some of them are just mean, and only want us around for what they can get from us. That's the kind of human you have." CB spoke softly and sincerely, wanting Storm to understand that he was trying to help.

"You are wrong CB. My human loves me." Storm growled.

"If he did, he would not be using you to steal from other humans, would not scream at you in anger because you didn't bring shiny baubles to him and certainly would not throw shoes at you, leading you to hide under a couch until he calmed down. And... for goodness sake, he definitely would not pick you up by your neck and scream in your face."

"It was my fault, I failed him in what I was told to do."

"Storm, a good human would never... I repeat, never... ask you to steal from other humans just to get what they want. Tell me something, Storm, do you know Kieko very well?" CB asked, changing the conversation and tone.

32

"What? Ummm... I know her pretty well, I guess, what does that have to do with anything?" Storm said, confusion curling his forehead.

"Kieko used to have a different human. In fact, she has had five different humans over the past two years. She is technically a dog for hire. She's big, strong and has an attitude as big as her giant fangs. But what she doesn't have, is a good human. She is hired by the worst of humans, to act as security for them as they do things that are wrong, dangerous and usually incredibly illegal. That's the kind of human you have. He is using you and will hurt you, or dispose of you, when you fail him."

"You don't know what you're talking about, CB. He's a good human, he just has a propensity for shiny things. That's not bad, just quirky. He would never hurt me. He loves me."

"Storm, I really need you to listen." CB said quietly.

"No, CB, I'm done listening. I'm going home, I've had enough of you for one day." as he said this he stood up and began walking away.

"Storm, please listen for one minute more." CB said as Storm stopped and turned back to him, "I will follow you back to your house tonight. It will be hard for me to get past Kieko to help you, but if you are in true danger, I'll do everything I can. Just think about something while we walk back. You know my past, and you know what I do now. I am doing anything I can to help both humans and animals, but I need help. The kind of help you can give."

"Why me? You have dozens of cats following you to help out. Surely, they have all the skills I have ." Storm said.

"True, some of the cats in my group are pretty skillful, and all of them work hard for me. But, what I really need is a partner who has the level of skill you have. Who can work with me, and eventually help me expand what we do. You have those skills. What I am asking is for you to leave a human who is harmful and join me and my group."

"Thanks, but my human loves me, I'll stay there." Storm said with finality.

"Fine, I'm just asking you to think about it." as they turned and began walking back to Deeter Street, CB leaned over and whispered softly in Storm's ear, "Let me just add one thing. You have mentioned several times how much your human loves you… but what you never have mentioned is… that you love him."

Six

Storm entered the house on Deeter Street through a small cat door that had been installed in the side door of the house. It was good to be home, he thought, even if it was a bit stressful from time to time. Today, though, he had a headache and was looking forward to a drink of water, perhaps a little food and a long nap.

Entering the kitchen, he noticed that both his water and food dishes were empty. With a shake of his head he turned and walked into the living room and headed for his favorite chair, a large soft overstuffed recliner. Oh, how great a nap was going to be. With a soft leap he jumped into the chair and settled into the corner. For a moment he allowed himself to think about CB.

What was the deal with that crazy old cat? He definitely had a purpose to his life, but what led him there? And for a cat who was obviously older and a bit overweight, how could he be so quiet and stealthy? Not to mention how he could possibly be so fast and strong. Never had Storm seen a fighter like CB before. He had skills, speed, agility, and more tricks at his command than Storm had ever imagined.

Storm lifted his paw and rubbed the side of his head. That head-butt move was stunning. How he had managed to stay alive from that shot to the head was beyond him. Yeah, that was something.

But at the same time, CB had this drive to take Storm away from everything he had ever known. He had been in this house since he was a kitten. He had learned his skills from an old cat that had lived here when he was growing into a juvenile, and finally a grown cat. Sure, he had a way to go to fill in and grow to his final full size, but he was certainly grown enough to handle himself.

So, why was CB working so hard to change things. And what had he meant by the question he had asked as they were walking? Of course his human loved him, what was CB getting at? What did he mean when he said that Storm had never said he loved his human? Of course he did, why wouldn't he? Yet... CB had an interesting point, Storm had never actually said he loved his human, and the question was... why not? He did, didn't he?

As he considered all this, he felt his eyes growing heavy and sleep beginning to overtake him. He was almost asleep when he heard his human enter the house. At least he would have fresh food and water when he woke up. It was then that he heard his human scream and he was jarred out of his reverie.

"Not again!" his human screamed, "There is no way that you came back here again with nothing to show me."

Storm looked up from his comfortable corner and stared at his human. Surely, he was not being yelled at again. He was tired, he had a headache, and he was worn out from fighting. He would gladly go out later and find something shiny, but for now, even the most dense of humans could see he was in bad shape and needed some rest.

"I told you not to fail me again." his human screamed, "What in the world would make you fail me again. Oh, I see, you have been fighting again, and you think that will get you out of your job. I have had enough of you, you worthless ball of fur." at this, Storm stared at his human, surely he wasn't seeing what he was seeing. He couldn't understand the words, of course, cats can't understand the human language, but his human was actually angry and didn't care that he had had a difficult day.

It was then that a book hit the chair not an inch from his head. With a screech, he jumped out of the corner of his chair and landed at a run heading for the couch. If he could crawl under, or behind, it he could wait until his human calmed down. But before he could reach the couch, while his human was venting his anger at the top of his voice, Storm felt the breeze of a knife blow past his ear. In absolute shock he dove under the couch just as the tip for the knife wedged into the arm of the couch.

As Storm was scrambling under the couch, and his human was moving forward, yelling at him for failing him, Storm saw a large mass of grey fly through the air and land, with all four sets of claws extended, and teeth bared, on his humans head.

CB! How in the world had CB gotten into the house? And why, he wondered quickly, would CB risk himself to help him? And what about Kieko, how had CB gotten past the giant dog? Then he noticed the open window.

While CB kept his human occupied, Storm ran from under the couch and dove through the open window, landing softly in the lawn. Seconds later CB followed him.

"Are you O.K.?" CB said as he landed.

"He threw a knife at me!" Storm gasped.

"I know, I'm sorry about that, I tried to get in sooner, but that crazy dog was being rather annoying. Are you alright, though?" CB said softly, trying to calm and sooth the small cat.

"HE THREW A KNIFE AT ME!! HE TRIED TO KILL ME!!!! What in the world was that all about?" Storm yelled.

As they stood trying to catch their breath, they heard Kieko's barking coming from around the front of the house, heading at them, "We need to move." CB said, "We can talk later."

With a leap they scaled the nearest tree and followed a long branch to where it hung over the fence. With a deft leap, they landed on the other side of the fence, just as Kieko reached the same spot on her side, "Don't show yourselves around here again. I swear, CB if you come back here again, I'll kill you." Kieko growled.

"Oh, we'll be back, Kieko. In the meantime, begin looking for a new human." CB replied.

"My current human is just fine, thank you very much. But I have had enough of you two. Come around here again and neither of you will survive."

"Well, thanks for the warning. We'll be leaving now. But, I expect we'll see each other soon."

"Then you will die, CB." Kieko snapped.

With a chuckle, CB and Storm turned and began walking back toward CB's alley. They walked in silence, as CB gave Storm some time to sort out what had just happened. This was a turning point in the young cats life and he needed to make sure the full impact of it sank in.

When they reached the small doorway with the recliner chair, at the far end of CB's alley, CB pushed a large pillow into a corner for Storm to lie down on, then hopped up into the chair and sat quietly watching the small cat. Storm was very quiet and seemed to be shaking slightly.

They sat this way for a few minutes before Storm said quietly, "You tried to warn me, but I wouldn't listen. I really thought he was a good human… but he tried to kill me. I don't really understand CB."

"Storm, you are a great cat. Or at least you have the makings of one. But, you just happen to have ended up with a bad human. He didn't care about you because of who you are, he only cared about you for what you could do for him. When you didn't give him what he wanted, he didn't see any further need for you. This is a huge loss for him, and a huge gain for you." CB watched the small cat and couldn't help but feel sorry for him.

"What do I do now, CB? I've never lived without a human before." Storm said quietly.

"Well, as I said before, if you are willing to work with me, I have need of a cat with all of your special talents." CB said.

"How can I be of help to a cat like you, who has so much strength and knowledge?"

"Well, you will need some training, of course. Many of the cats here are hard workers, yet, most of them are lacking the knowledge and skill you have. You have learned to think fast, be creative, use your size and speed to your benefit and above all, you are incredibly smart. That's what we need. Stick with me and I'll make sure you are safe and… well… maybe we can do some good together."

"Fine, we'll give it a try… what do we do first?" Storm said.

"Well, first, we get you some food, water and sleep. Then," CB said with a sly smile, "we figure out a way to put your ex-human into the hands of the human legal system."

"Now, that... is something I think I can definitely get behind." Storm laughed.

Seven

Jaffa burst out laughing as CB explained his plan. Where in the world did this crazy old cat come up with his ideas?

"What a great plan… this is going to be fun. Though, I am extremely concerned for Storm. He could get killed."

"I know, Jaffa, I have the same concern, in fact I refused to agree to his part of the plan, unfortunately, he is right. It is the best part of the plan, it will solidify that his old human ends up in the hands of the authorities." CB said softly. It wasn't too late to change the plan, but unfortunately, Storm was right about this. The trick was going to be keeping Storm alive long enough to get through it.

"O.k., Jaffa, you know the plan. Get the human police from their station at sunset, and we'll see what we can do to help out." CB said.

"When will Storm be finished with his part of the plan?" Jaffa asked with true concern in his voice.

"I'm not sure, he's there now, if things work out he'll be in and out in about ten minutes. I'm heading there now, to see what I can do to help. For now, we'll just have to be patient and see what happens." CB said before giving Jaffa a soft head butt and heading down the street.

* * *

Storm stood on the corner post of the house on Deeter St. He had not been back to the house since his human had tried to kill him. He could see Keiko resting quietly by the front door. With a deep sigh, he realized the burden ahead of him. He needed to get past Keiko and into the house, take what he needed from the house and get back out again. All without getting killed by either the big Akita, or by his former human.

Taking a deep breath and letting it out slowly, he looked closely at the building in front of him. He couldn't get in through the front door, and the window at the side of the house, which both he and CB had escaped through previously, was closed. That only left the small basement window at the back of the house. The window had been broken several months earlier when a branch broke off an old oak tree during a storm. His human had never bothered to look for damage after the storm and never noticed the broken window.

With a quick glance over his shoulder Storm noticed that the sun was beginning to set, and he knew CB would be there in a few minutes to set the plan in motion. As he started moving down the fence toward the back window, he heard Keiko yelling loudly and he knew CB had arrived.

With Keiko's attention concentrated elsewhere, Storm knew it was time to move. Crouching low, he ran as fast as he could down the fence until he got to the window. Then, throwing all caution to the wind, he dove for the window. He cleared the broken shards by millimeters and landed softly in the basement, just as he heard Keiko screeched, "CB GET OFF MY PROPERTY… I TOLD YOU I'D KILL YOU IF YOU CAME HERE AGAIN." Storm couldn't hear anything after that and had to trust that CB knew what he was doing.

Hurdle one passed. Now came the hard part.
Creeping through the dark basement, Storm headed for
the stairs. He knew that the latch on the door at the top of
the stairs was broken and he would be able to get into the
main part of the house with no problem. What was a
problem was knowing that his old human was home and
he would need to get past him.

Slowly, he climbed the stairs, making sure he
avoided the squeaking third stair, until he reached the top.
He put his ear against the closed door and listened closely.
He could hear his human yelling at someone, but he
couldn't tell where in the house he was. He was yelling so
loud that the sound could have been coming from
anywhere. Taking a deep breath he used his head to
slowly push the door open enough to slide his head
through, while keeping his muscles tensed to jump and run
if needed.

Peeking around the edge of the door, Storm saw
that the kitchen and hallway were both clear. The sound of
yelling continued, but he could now tell it was in the living
room… the exact room he needed to be in.

* * *

CB strolled calmly up to the front gate. His main
goal at this point was to get Keiko's attention focused
anywhere but where Storm was. As he reached the gate,
he saw Keiko jump up from her position at the front door.
At first, she was screaming so incoherently that he couldn't
understand anything she said. Then he heard her yell, "CB
GET OFF MY PROPERTY… I TOLD YOU I'D KILL YOU IF
YOU CAME HERE AGAIN.", and he knew he had

accomplished his goal. Storm was free to get past her now and CB had no way to help him any further.

"Oh, please, Keiko," CB said softly, "how exactly are you planning to kill me?" with a swagger he strolled over to the gate and jumped up on it, "You know I'm faster and more agile than you are. You can't catch me, and if you did I will guarantee that with my claws being as sharp as they are, your eyes and nose would be shredded."

"I may be shredded, but you'd be dead. Pretty fair trade, as far as I'm concerned." Keiko screeched, "At least you will be out of my life."

"Keiko, I know you hate these little talks, but you need to know that in about ten minutes, you are going to be short another human. He'll be going to jail and you will be seeking another reprobate to hire you. Don't worry, I won't tell your new human how incompetent you are as a guard dog." with a smile and a chuckle, CB stopped and looked over at Keiko. He could tell that the big dog was torn between trying to rush at him, and indeed started to do so, and stopping to figure out what he had just heard. Ultimately, he stopped.

"Wait… what?" Keiko said with some consternation.

"What… what, Keiko?" CB Laughed.

"What do you mean I will be without a human in about ten minutes?" Keiko asked.

"Well," CB said calmly, "you see… right now, Storm is in the house stealing back some of the baubles he stole for your human over the past couple months. And another friend of ours is working on leading the human police to this house. Let's see what they have to say about finding a whole pile of stolen jewelry on your human's property."

Keiko stared at CB for a second, then let out a scream and ran toward the front door. She had to let her human know what was happening before it was too late. Just as she got to the front door it flew open and her human came rushing out of the door screaming at the top of his voice and threw a shoe at her. The point was clear… SHUT UP! but Keiko knew she couldn't be quiet now, she had to get into the house and stop that stupid cat. Without thinking further, she rushed the front door, knocked her human out of the way and ran into the house.

* * *

Jaffa waited until the sun was just beginning to set, then turned and headed toward the human police station. A block away, he heard Keiko, the gigantic Akita, begin to screech. It was time.

Walking quickly along the front wall of the building, he soon saw what he was looking for, a human police officer sitting at his desk doing some form of paperwork. After a quick chuckle at what he was about to do, he looked at the small diamond and gold bracelet he had brought from his own home. If all went well, it would be returned to his humans before they realized it was gone. Then, clearing his throat to make sure he was in his best voice, he began to howl like his tail was on fire.

Inside the building, the human police officer jumped at the sound and spun around in his seat to look out the window. When Jaffa was sure he had the officers attention, he picked the bracelet up in his mouth and started waving it around. The officer, being a very smart man, immediately realized what he was seeing. Here was a cat with a diamond bracelet in its mouth. Since there had been a rash of jewelry stolen around town lately, the officer quickly added two and two and came up with four. As the officer jumped out of his chair and started running toward the front door, he yelled to a couple of his other officers to follow him.

Jaffa, seeing that the first part of his goal was accomplished began running toward the house on Deeter Street. At first, in his excitement, he ran as fast as he could, but quickly realized he was much faster than the humans and slowed down until the humans were close behind him. Then, waving the bracelet as a reminder, he ran directly toward the house.

* * *

Storm watched the two humans in the living room. The argument was escalating and his former human was getting red in the face, screaming obscenities at the other man in the room. Outside, he could hear Keiko getting increasingly upset and her barking getting louder. When it reached its maximum, the two men in the living room broke off their argument and turned to look at the front door. His old human yelled something at Keiko, moved to the door, and bent down to grab an old shoe lying in the corner.

As the man rushed off toward the door, Storm saw just what he needed, that the two humans were distracted. He rushed out of his hiding spot and over to a cabinet in the corner of the room. Quickly nosing open the door of the cabinet, Storm grabbed the string on an old cloth bag inside. The bag, he knew, contained all the jewelry his human had used him to steal.

Turning from his position, he saw the two humans still focused on the front door. He saw the human open the front door and throw the shoe at Keiko. A second later he saw the giant dog rush past the man, almost knocking him over, and barge into the house. As Keiko ran in, Storm ran toward the door. Just as he got to where the big dog was, with jaws snapping, he saw the human straighten up, standing in the middle of the door facing into the yard. With all his strength, Storm ran and jumped. He cleared the snapping jaws by a fraction of an inch, bent his head down, still with the bag in his mouth and hit his former human squarely between the shoulder blades with his shoulder.

* * *

CB looked over his shoulder, just as the front door opened and the man came out on the porch to throw the shoe at Keiko. He saw Jaffa, just across the street, running toward the house with a bracelet hanging out of his mouth. Behind Jaffa were three of the human police officers. Turning back to the house, he saw Keiko rush past the man at the door and without hesitation, he rushed toward the man. When he was about three feet away, CB jumped with all his strength, lowered his head and hit the man squarely in the chest with his shoulder... at exactly the same instant that Storm hit the man in the back.

There was a sickening crunching sound and CB knew the man had broken at least three ribs when the power of the two cats collided. With a scream, the man crumbled to the ground, holding his ribs. CB and Storm stood up at the same time and CB saw Storm rush out into the yard, just as the human police came running through the gate.

Seeing what was going on, the officers immediately realized they were looking at a situation that would solve a couple dozen unsolved crimes. In front of them was a cat dumping out a bag of jewelry on the ground and a man, who was well known to them from previous crimes, writhing on the ground. Not even bothering to take his pain into account, they quickly handcuffed the man, picked up the jewelry and hauled the man off.

Jaffa, meanwhile, sat by the gate with his humans bracelet in his mouth, completely forgotten by the human police. With a laugh, he waved at CB and Storm and rushed off back home to return the bracelet before his humans missed it.

Eight

As the police officers took the man away, Storm and CB began walking back to the alley. On their way, they stopped at Jaffa's home and thanked him again for all his help. He had made it back to his home and replaced the bracelet with no problems whatsoever.

"You really were a great help, Jaffa." CB said with obvious respect in his voice, "You may not be the biggest cat in the city, but no one has a bigger heart. You should be very proud of yourself."

Jaffa smiled at such a great compliment from such a powerful cat, "Aw, heck, CB... I didn't do much. But, I'm glad I could do what I could. What will you do now?"

"Well, we'll head back to the alley and see what other problems are awaiting our help."

"If there is ever anything I can do to help out, just don't hesitate to ask." Jaffa said.

"We will absolutely keep you in mind, and don't be a stranger. The alley is always home to you. For now, go inside and enjoy the love and comfort of your humans. Thanks again, you are a great little guy, and an excellent new friend." CB and Storm gave Jaffa a soft headbutt and turned again toward their home in the alley.

"He is a great little guy, isn't he? Funny how so much strength can come in such a small bundle." Storm said quietly.

"Agreed, Storm. I look forward to watching him grow. Of course, I look forward to seeing where you end up as well." CB said with a glance over at his friend.

"Well, I think we both know I've turned a big corner in my behavior. You and I are a team now, so let's see what good work we can do." Storm said as they strolled calmly down the road.

* * *

"Can I ask you another question, CB?" Storm asked after a few minutes of silence.

"Sure." CB said.

"Well, actually two questions. Not long after we first met I made a comment to you that it was too bad you have never had a human who cared about you. First of all, I need to apologize, that was rude of me. But, even though you didn't think I could hear you, you responded, 'Oh, how wrong you are'. Did you have a human once? And if so, and if he cared for you, and you cared for him, why do you use CB as your name and not the name he called you?" Storm asked.

"You really have amazing hearing, don't you? I'll have to keep that in mind." for a moment, CB stared off into the distance as if his mind were somewhere other than where his body was, "Someday, I will tell you that story, Storm, but not now. For now, that pain is more than I care to deal with. For now, just accept me for what I am, and consider this issue closed."

"O.k., CB, I won't pry. You're secrets are yours. How about we find some food and water?"

With a laugh, CB nudged Storm with his shoulder. "Great idea, Storm. The sun won't be up for a while yet, so I know a place we can get some fish from yesterdays catch that the humans won't be paying attention to."

They trotted off in the direction of the docks, laughing and telling jokes to each other. But all the while, one thought kept running through Storm's mind… "Sure," he thought to himself, "I'll accept him for who he is… but this issue is far from being closed!!"

The Cat Burglar:
Paradise Lost

One

"So, CB," Storm said quietly, "ummm... who is that beautiful, young Blue Point Siamese I saw roaming around here yesterday?"

CB chuckled, "So... you noticed her, did you?" he looked over at Storm with a smile creasing his muzzle. Hmmm... he thought to himself, that's not a bad match.

"Well," Storm said with an embarrassed quiver in his voice, "I guess it would have been a bit difficult to miss her. She's really quite lovely." Storm had seen the beautiful cream colored cat, with the faint blue-grey tints on her face, ears, tail and legs, strolling through the alley with CB the day before, when he returned from an errand CB had sent him on.

"I agree, she's a stunner. Her name is Ginka,"CB said pronouncing it with a J sound, "she's a friend of Jaffa's from over in The Heights. He thought she might be able to help us out with some information about that group of cats causing problems down at the docks. Her information was great, I passed it along to Rocky and Herbie who are working down there, and we may be on the way to shutting them down."

"Excellent news. Those guys down at the docks have been a pain, it would be good to shut them down. As far as Ginka is concerned, well…" Storm said distractedly, "maybe I'll have to get Jaffa to introduce me."

CB laughed softly, "You do that, Storm. In the meantime…"

At this point their conversation was cut short by the sound of a cat screaming in the alley.

"CB HELP!! SHE'S GONE!! HELP!!" the cat yelled, "HELP, CB, STORM!! SOMEONE TOOK HER, HURRY!!"

As CB and Storm sat up in their seats in the small entryway of the building they called their home, they saw Jaffa come running around the corner out of breath.

"CB, STORM… HELP, THEY TOOK HER, SHE'S MISSING, HURRY!!" Jaffa yelled.

"Jaffa," CB said quietly, "slow down. What are you talking about?"

"They took her, she's missing, you have to hurry and help." Jaffa huffed.

"Jaffa… stop babbling, take a deep breath, gather your thoughts and tell us what you are talking about." CB said with a touch of exasperation.

At this, Jaffa stopped, closed his eyes and got his breathing under control, "Paradise." he said, "She's missing. Someone took her."

"WHAT?? WHEN?? WHERE??" CB yelled as he jumped out of his chair and began running down the alley.

"Just a little while ago. She was at the show, down at the Civic Center and she disappeared. Someone took her... she's been kidnapped." Jaffa said as he ran.

Storm rushed to catch up with the two cats who had apparently gone completely insane, "Wait, what the heck are you two talking about? Who's 'Paradise'?"

"That's right, I forgot, you were raised in a house without other cats, you wouldn't know who she is." CB said, "Paradise is a show cat... considered by some to be the most beautiful cat currently alive. She's a Persian, about my size... fairly large for a female, but with amazingly well groomed, long white fur. She's incredible. I met her a few years ago in... well... in another part of my life. We need to find her."

With that explanation, the three friends rushed down the alley in the direction of the Civic Center.

Two

The Civic Center is on the east side of town, just on the edge of what the humans call "downtown". It is the oldest part of town, and consists of streets filled with shops, offices and markets.

On this morning, the parking lot of the Civic Center was filled with cars belonging to the people with cats participating in the annual Cat Show, and people coming to watch. This show, which had been an annual event for longer than any cat living could remember, was a highlight of the year. It was a time when all the most remarkable cats in the region gathered to be judged (by the humans, not by other cats) to see who was the most beautiful, largest, best groomed, most true to their breed and a dozen other categories.

The cats who were performing, or being judged, seemed to love the attention and being able to brag about their rankings for the next year. These were not the workaday cats that CB and Storm hung out with. These were the most aesthetic and pampered of cats. Though, annually, comments were passed around that if CB was better groomed and not living in an alley, he would certainly be in the running for several awards.

As CB, Storm and Jaffa got to the woods in the park at the edge of the parking lot surrounding the Civic Center, they stopped out of sight behind a bush to review the situation.

"The first problem is that we're cats. A bunch of cats, going into a building with a bunch of people showing cats is going to be a big issue. They are going to think we got loose from our cages and need to be taken back." CB said.

"Ummm," Storm said, "cages??? What cages??"

"Wow, we really need to get you up to speed here, don't we?" Jaffa said, "These are show cats. Their humans pamper them beyond belief, they have to be fed, exercised and groomed in exactly the most specific ways. They aren't allowed to roam free around the Civic Center. They are brought in cages… or what they call 'carriers', and are only taken out when it is their time to be shown."

"O.k., I get that… but it seems a bit barbaric, doesn't it?" Storm said.

"Well, yeah, but these cats love it. They are all about the attention. And no one gets the attention that these cats do." Jaffa laughed.

"So… not your everyday working class cats, huh? Alright. And I take it that this 'Paradise' is the best of the best, right?" Storm asked.

"Yep… what they call 'Best in Show'. There's no one like Paradise."

CB, who had been listening quietly, nodded calmly, "No doubt about it, there's nobody like Paradise. Which means, there is no target bigger than Paradise. Any human wanting to have the best cat in the show will want her."

"Perhaps more importantly, anyone who wants the best cat in the show and doesn't have her, will do anything necessary to get rid of her." Storm said.

CB and Jaffa looked at him with shock on their faces, "Wow, you really do learn quickly, don't you? That's completely correct. No one would want her for who she is, they could never show her because she's too famous. So, it has to be someone who has a cat who may be a runner up and is tired of being a runner up. Someone wants to win and is very tired of losing." CB said.

"So, what do we do, CB?" Jaffa asked.

"Well," Storm said, "it seems to me that we have a human element to deal with here. Certainly a cat couldn't take another cat out from under the watchful eyes of the humans. It has to be humans who took her."

"I agree. Here we go again. There are great humans, there are good humans and there are the not so great humans." CB said gravely, "Ultimately, we are going to need the human police again. Which, I think we can leave to the humans who Paradise lives with. Certainly, they have already called in the police. But, whoever took her has certainly left the area by now. Paradise can't still be in this building."

"Absolutely, I agree completely." Storm said, "But, one of the cats in that building may have seen something. We need to get in and ask some questions. Without getting caught, of course."

"Jaffa, you know these cats better than we do. Do you have any idea who the closest runner ups would be? And, maybe where they might live?" CB asked.

"I know a couple of them, but I can go ask Ginka, she follows this stuff more closely than I do."

"Excellent, between the two of you, try to come up with the names and locations of… say, the top five cats under Paradise in rankings for Best in Show. From there, check out their homes and see if there is any action going on there. The humans those cats live with will be here with their cats. But, if one of them had Paradise kidnapped, there may be activity at their home… or some property affiliated with them. Can you do that?" Storm asked.

"Sure, no problem. We'll get right on it. We'll meet you back here in an hour, will that work?" Jaffa asked.

"Perfect. We'll be here." with the plan set, Jaffa ran off in the direction of The Heights.

Three

"O.k., Storm. Where do we go from here? We need to get into that building, talk to some cats and get back out, without getting caught and put in a cage ourselves." CB said.

"Well, first of all, I think we need to split up. One of us getting caught is a problem, both of us getting caught is a full blown concern."

"Agreed. Do you know anything about this building?"

"Yeah. I used to do a little 'business' here for my previous human. Anytime you have a lot of people in one place jewelry tends to break, drop off, get laid down and not picked up, you know the game. So, I would just come here, look around and pick up what I could find."

CB burst out laughing, "Oh, my goodness, Storm. I used to do the exact same thing when I was in the same 'business' that you were in. That is too funny." even though the situation was very serious, they took a minute to laugh over the old times.

"Okay, our best chance to get in is the old ventilation unit at the back of the building. It's been a few months since I have been here, but I am sure they haven't changed it. Once we get in, there is a hole about twenty feet down the vent that opens into a conference room. From there we can get into the main hall." Storm said.

"Alright, once we get into the hall, stay hidden as much as you can, but talk to every cat you run across. Any information we can get would be great."

"If we can get it weeded down to three or four candidates, we may have something to go on." Storm said.

"Sounds good, Storm. Let's go".

* * *

Staying in the shadows as long as possible, CB and Storm moved swiftly around the building until they reached the old ventilation system at the back. The Civic Center was an old building, and long past the point of needing to be replaced. Rather than fix the old building, the humans had apparently made the decision to build a new center. Since the new building was already in process, it was just a matter of time before this old relic was torn down.

The metal cover on the old ventilation system was hanging by one screw, in the upper right corner. Storm reached out with his left paw and pushed the cover open. Quickly, he and CB jumped in and began creeping down the dark tubing. As Storm had said, there was a hole in the tubing twenty feet down, covered on the outside by a grate. CB reached the opening first and stood quietly listening. After a few moments of not hearing anything, he pushed the grate off and they slipped through the hole, into the conference room.

The room was large and dark and the door on the far side was opened wide. The two friends ran to the door and looked out. In front of them was the main display room of the Civic Center, and in that room were hundreds of people, with hundreds of cats. The sounds and scents were staggering.

"Wow!" CB said, "I never realized just how overwhelming this place would be."

"No kidding!! This is nuts, we'll never learn anything here."

"Well, let's try anyway. You go left, I'll go right and we'll meet back here in fifteen minutes."

"Sounds great."

"Oh, and Storm." CB said

"Yeah?"

"Don't get caught."

"Good plan."

With that exchange, the two friends headed out in their opposite directions.

* * *

Storm came out into the main hall on the end farthest from what he would learn later was the judging station. The humans were all watching the judges and not really paying attention to what was going on around them. Storm strolled up to the first cat he saw and caught their attention.

"Excuse me." he said softly, so the humans wouldn't hear him, "I hear that Paradise is missing, did you see anything?"

The cat, a large Calico, looked at him with disdain. "Really, what would a squat little cat like you be doing here?" she said with a sniff and a shake of her head.

"Wow!" Storm said, "That's really the way you start a conversation?"

"You should be impressed that I even bother to talk to you at all. We obviously aren't the same level of cat, now are we?"

Storm burst out laughing, "No, we aren't. And thank goodness for that."

With that, he moved on to the next cat... and had an almost identical conversation. This went on for cat after cat. Just as he was getting annoyed with these cats, he heard a commotion on the opposite side of the hall, and saw CB come flying over a stack of cages, with two humans running after him.

Storm immediately started running toward them. As he reached where CB and his chasers were, he dove at the feet of the nearest human and knocked him over. CB spun around and hit the legs of the other human, sending him flying. As he and Storm came together, they saw half a dozen other humans heading at them.

CB looked at Storm and said, "This is completely worthless, let's get out of here, we're wasting time."

As quickly as possible, they rushed back to the conference room, into the ventilation system and out of the Civic Center.

"What a bunch of worthless, self-centered, over fluffed furballs! I talked to a bunch of them, and none of could even hold a hint of a conversation." Storm yelled when they reached the park.

"I couldn't agree more." CB said. "I had the same experience. They couldn't even see past their own fur long enough to know that Paradise was missing. We need a different approach."

"Let's go see if we can find out what Jaffa and Ginka have learned." Storm said, "Maybe they have a clue for us."

"Yeah, let's go, I can't deal with this place any longer." Storm said in a huff, an with that the two friends started running toward The Heights.

Four

They found Jaffa and Ginka huddled by the large oak tree just outside Jaffa's apartment, chatting quietly. When they saw CB and Storm run up, they jumped and stared. The first thing they noticed was that both of the friends looked angry.

"CB, what's wrong? You guys look furious. We were just going over our findings before coming to you." Jaffa asked quickly.

"Pampered, puffed up pieces of fancy fur." Storm growled.

"Storm, relax. You're going to have an aneurism." CB laughed, "Let's just say the cats at the show weren't very helpful."

"Oh, I'm sorry to hear that." Ginka said softly, "I was really hoping we would learn something there."

"Well, it is what it is." CB said philosophically, "All right what else do we know? Have you learned anything."

"Well," Jaffa said, "maybe we can be of some help. Ginka, let them know what we know."

"Okay, well... it turns out there are four cats who are true contenders. Two are from a different city, and have not been in this competition before, so I think we can rule them out. The other two are local. One lives up in The Willows. The other lives in Jones." Ginka explained.

"JONES?" Storm and CB said in unison, "Who would have a cat like that in Jones? That's a rough part of town."

Jaffa looked at each them in turn, cleared his throat and said softly, "Ummm... that was kind of scary, I think you two are spending too much time together! You're talking in unison." this led to a bout of laughter as they all let the stress of the last half hour slip away, "Anyway, we wondered the same thing so we went over to have a look around, and guess what we found?"

"Let me guess... a whole bunch of activity. There shouldn't be, they should be at the show." CB said.

"Well, no, actually something else." Jaffa said with a smile, "Something gigantic, with long black and white fur, and an attitude beyond belief."

"KEIKO!!!" CB and Storm screamed in unison.

"Ummm, yeah." Ginka said, "But you two need to stop that, it's scary." again the four broke into a fit of laughter.

Finally, CB got them settled down, "Alright, then, we know where Paradise is. Wherever Keiko is, problems are, and some human with an angle."

"On that we are all agreed." Storm said, "I'm beginning to think that we should start all of our investigations by looking for Keiko. What I don't get is why the humans would be interested. What would they gain?"

"Oh, that's easy. Money. Storm, you already learned from your past human that some humans are obsessed with money. Well, the winner of Best in Show makes a ton of money. We're talking a big incentive here." CB explained.

"Alright, I get that. Then I guess we need to head down to Jones and have a chat with a massive, bad tempered mutt." Storm said with a chuckle. This was going to be fun... all of CB's cases were fun... if a bit dangerous at times.

"What can we do to help." Jaffa asked.

"For now," CB replied, "you can head back to your nice homes and get some rest, you have had a big day. I also hear your humans have adopted a little sister for you, Ginka. You should make sure she feels welcome. We'll take over for now and give you a holler if we need help."

"Oh, yeah, my new sister. Wait until you meet her, she's beautiful. Her name is Marti, you're going to love her, she's so sweet. I think Jaffa is already quite smitten." Ginka chuckled.

"Well... ummm... I... uh... you know, she's... well, she's really cute." Jaffa stammered.

Again, they all burst out laughing. "You know, Jaffa," CB said, "If you ever overcome that shyness, you are going to be quite a cat. Come on Storm, we have work to do." and with that the two friends started running toward Jones.

Five

There are parts of Jones that are considered the worst of the worst in human terms. They are run down, dark and exceedingly dangerous. CBs alley was in one of the seedier parts of Jones, and was generally considered off limits to most humans, but was perfect for the cats.

The house they were seeking, however, was in one of the better areas of Jones. The people in the area overall took care of their homes, kept their lawns trimmed and put a fresh coat of paint on the house fairly regularly. These were not slums, but they were definitely the homes of people who made a limited income and needed to spend it wisely.

It was a small, singe level house which, they would learn later, had three small bedrooms, a bath, a living room and an eat-in kitchen. Like most of the other homes in the neighborhood, it was well kept and even had a small rose garden in the back yard. The wooden post fence was painted the same deep beige color as the house. Ultimately, CB thought as he looked at it, this is a house owned by someone who cares. Unfortunately, if they were involved in the kidnapping of Paradise, what they cared about was money... making enough of it to get out of the neighborhood. An admirable goal, if one doesn't succumb to breaking the law to achieve it.

"Nice place." Storm said as they approached, "Definitely beats the heck out where I grew up."

"I agree completely. It's going to be sad if this turns out to be the place we are looking for."

At this, Storm saw the opening he had been seeking to re-approach an old conversation, "So," Storm said with a smile, "is this pretty similar to the house you grew up in with your human?"

"I told you we were done with that conversation, Storm. Leave it alone."

"Sure, CB. But, I just don't get it. You claim to have had a great human, who loved you and who you loved, but you refuse to talk about him... or her... and won't use the name they gave you. Why?"

"Drop it, Storm!" CB said with irritation, "That part of my life is too painful. I'm not talking about it." for a moment, CB looked off into the distance, and was silent. This darned cat isn't going to give up on this, is he? CB thought. Maybe, someday, we'll get to that, but not now.

"Okay, okay, fine. But we aren't done with this." Storm smiled to himself.

Slowly, they approached the fence, and were on the verge of hopping up onto the gate, when they were cut short by a low growl.

"Oh, no... that crazy dog again." Storm said with a sigh.

"She's not crazy Storm."

"Okay, maybe not, just mean."

"Oh." CB said, "I'm not sure about that either. I really think she's just a good dog in a bad situation."

"Really? Well, she's been in that same bad situation half a dozen times now. There must be something they see in her." Storm said with a chuckle.

"I hear you, Storm, there seems to be something there. But, I can't help but think that with a little help, we might get somewhere with her."

"You know, I can't argue with you, you saw something in me, that others didn't. But if she really is a good dog, why is she always at the homes we have problems with?" Storm looked over at CB and saw his brow furl.

"Well, this is going to sound a bit odd, but Keiko is an Akita. They are working dogs. Her breed was designed and bred specifically for guarding things. It's the work she does. So, in order to work, she needs a job. And with her size and strength, anyone looking to do things that need serious guarding, are going to find her to be the perfect fit."

"So what can we do to help?" Storm asked.

"I'm not completely sure yet. But, I have an idea." CB said. The trick, he thought, is getting her to want help.

"What are you two doing here? There's nothing illegal going on here, these are nice people." Keiko said with a growl.

"We seriously hope you are right, Keiko. Unfortunately, we aren't so sure." CB said. He could see frustration building up in the giant dog. She really seemed to think she was in a good place.

"Leave me alone CB, I finally found a good place, don't ruin it for me."

"Keiko." Storm said, "We really want this to be a good place for you, and want you to be happy, but we think there is a problem here."

Keiko growled lowly. She could not believe this was happening again. Was this never going to end? "Darnit, guys. There is just me, a cat and my two humans here. They are nice, not like the others. They work real jobs, take care of their house, and are good to me and the cat. What more do you want?"

"Well, the cat is kind of the point. What kind of cat is it?" CB asked.

"Ummm... well, I think she's a Maine Coon. As cats go, I guess she's pretty."

"Is she award winning pretty?" Storm asked.

"Ummm... yeah, I guess so. Though, I don't know if she's as pretty as the new one they brought home this morning, that one is a real looker. Why, what does that matter?" Keiko said in confusion.

Storm and CB exchanged a sad look. CB let out a low sigh and turned to the big dog, "This new cat... is she, by any chance, a large white Persian?"

"I'm not sure, I don't know cats that well, but she is white and has a smushed in face. Is that a Persian?" Keiko asked.

"Yeah, Keiko, it is." Storm said. He looked over at CB, cleared his throat and said softly, "And this particular white Persian just happens to be a Grand Champion by the name of Paradise. She was stolen from the cat show this morning."

For a moment, Keiko did nothing other than stare at the two cats. Then, with a growl, she launched into a tirade of incoherent screaming. When her frustration wore off, she looked at the two cats, and said angrily, "What, exactly, are you planning to do?"

"We are planning to set her free, and have your humans placed in jail." CB said.

"You know I can't allow that. This is my job." Keiko said.

"Keiko, this cat belongs to someone else. Someone who is desperate to get her back. We need to make that happen, with your help, or without it." CB said softly.

"You need to leave now. That cat is my responsibility until my humans get back. If you try to get in here, my teeth and claws will have to do their jobs." Keiko growled.

"Well, we're going to have to take that chance." CB said.

"How?"

"I'm not sure yet, we'll be back when we think of what we are going to do." Storm said with a laugh. "Come on CB, we need to go."

CB stared at him as if he had lost his mind. "Storm, we aren't leaving here until we have Paradise, and can return her safely."

"Nope... we're leaving now." Storm said with a chuckle, "Come on, off we go."

As Storm started to leave, CB glanced over at Keiko, and they exchanged a look of confusion, "Yeah." Keiko said with a growl, "You better go, before your buddy gets too far away."

CB shook his head and ran off after Storm.

Six

"Have you lost your mind? We can't just leave her there." CB said when he caught up with Storm.

"Oh, no, quite the opposite. I figured out how we are going to solve the problem." Storm laughed.

"And how, exactly, are you going to do that?" CB asked.

"You're going to love this. Let me explain." and with that, Storm launched into his explanation.

* * *

Ten minutes later, CB once again stood by the gate at the small house in Jones, with Keiko making threats.

"I told you, CB, I can't let you in here, I have a job to do."

"I know, Keiko, so I'm not going to do anything. I'll just sit here and chat with you." CB smirked.

"Uhhh, okay, umm... how is that going to help you get this cat of yours back?" Keiko asked.

"Well, Keiko, you see we actually have a whole series of problems here. We need to get Paradise back to her owners, we need to get your humans into the hands of the authorities, and we need to find a way to help you." CB said.

"Help me? I don't need help."

"Oh, yeah you do. Unless you really want to spend the rest of your life working for the worst humans imaginable."

"I'm a working dog. This is my job, it's what I do."
Keiko said hesitantly.

"Fine, but does working have to necessarily mean
illegal?"

"Do you have something else in mind?"

"Well, actually, I do." CB replied. At that moment he
saw Storm come flying out of a side window of the house,
with a diamond collar in his mouth. Keiko saw storm out of
the corner of her eye and with scream, turned and ran after
him, but it was too late, Storm had already jumped over the
fence and was heading down the street. Keiko turned to
yell at CB, but he was gone. In all her frustration, Keiko let
out a scream at the top of her voice.

* * *

When they had been talking to Keiko earlier, Storm
had noticed that there was a small window on the side of
the house, which was partially open. There wasn't a
screen on the window and he knew that if he could get to it
without Keiko seeing him, he could get into the house, and
talk to Paradise. He and CB had figured out that they
really didn't need to free Paradise, as long as she wasn't
being harmed. They really didn't think she would be in
danger. These people were, ultimately, cat lovers. They
weren't going to harm her.

So, while CB was chatting with Keiko, Storm snuck
around to the side of the house. As before, he found the
window open, and while Keiko's back was to him, he ran
up and jumped through the window.

He landed in a small bedroom, with what appeared
to be a child's bed in it. Keiko hadn't mentioned a child in

the house, but he had no idea how old these humans were, maybe they had grandchildren who visited from time to time. Either way, it didn't matter. What was important was finding Paradise. He began walking down the hallway, and saw a second bedroom. And there, in a small plastic cage, was Paradise.

"Hi. My name is Storm, you must be Paradise. Are you o.k.?" he said as he entered the room.

"Yes, I'm fine. Just a bit cramped, this carrier is smaller than the one I usually use. Are you here to get me out?" Paradise asked.

"Well, that really depends. If you are in danger, or are being hurt, then yes, I am here to get you out. If not, we have a plan to not only get you out, but to get the humans here into the hands of the law."

"Well, that certainly sounds interesting. I would love to see these people arrested. What do you have in mind?" Paradise said with determination.

"What I would like is your collar. Is there any way you can get it off? With it, my partner and I have a plan."

"Who's your partner." Paradise asked.

"He's known as The Cat Burglar... or CB." Storm said.

"You are CB's partner? I had heard he had finally found a cat with just the right set of skills. You must be amazingly talented."

"Well, he thinks so. Personally, I think I have a lot to learn. So, you know CB?"

"Yes, we are old friends. If he has a plan, I am more than willing to go along with it. What can I do?"

"Thanks for helping out. For now, all we are going to ask for is your collar. Can you get it off?"

"Yes, I can. My owners don't like to have it mess my fur up, so they keep it loose. What are you going to do with it?" Paradise asked. While she got her collar off, Storm explained the plan. Then, with a quick goodbye, he ran back through the house and dove out the window he had come in.

As he hit the ground, Keiko saw him and turned and yelled at him, but by then he was over the fence and heading down the street. The last thing he heard was Keiko scream in frustration.

Seven

CB and Storm sat quietly in the park on the edge of the parking lot near the Civic Center. Most of the cars were gone, and it was clear that the cat show had been cancelled. The police cars were still there, as was the car which appeared to belong to Paradise's humans. The police, and Paradise's humans were standing by the main entrance talking.

"Well," Storm said with a chuckle, "it looks like we need to get this collar over to those humans."

"Yep. Though, it's not like we haven't played this game before." CB laughed.

"So, do you want to distract, or run?" Storm chuckled.

"Oh, heck, at my age, I'm more of a distractor, than a runner. That's why I trained someone young like you. You get to do all the hard work." CB smiled.

"Alright, I could use some exercise anyway. Rocky and Herbie have been meeting me at that fish place on the dock pretty regularly lately, I'm gaining weight."

"You ought to take Ginka there, I bet she loves sea food." CB laughed.

"I might just do that. Maybe a bit of mackerel, or some calamari. But, first things first. We need to get Paradise out of that house and back to her humans." the look on Storm's face suddenly shifted from joking to serious. He glanced over at CB and saw that he now had that same look.

"I'm ready when you are." CB said.

"Let's go."

***

Storm slowly walked out into the parking lot and headed toward the group of humans gathered by the door. When he got to within ten feet of the group, he glanced back at CB and gave him a quick nod. CB, suppressing a laugh, let out a screech as loud as he could. It sounded like a car had parked on his tail. He hissed and spat and generally sounded like he had completely lost his mind. Storm, ten feet from CB burst out laughing.

Meanwhile, the humans gathered by the door spun in unison and stared at the cat who sounded like he was stuck in a combine, their mouths agape and their eyes wide. Not sure what to do, they were starting to move toward him, when they saw Storm, barely ten feet away from them, waving a diamond collar. It took Paradise's humans just seconds to realize what they were seeing. They had bought that collar. They knew who it belonged to and they started running toward him. Storm saw them heading toward him and started running.

While one of the police officers got into the car to follow the others, Paradise's humans, and the other police officer followed Storm. Meanwhile, CB began running to catch up with the others, and the chase was on.

***

Storm started running and soon realized he was outpacing the humans. The police officer was in the lead, with the wife of Paradise's humans coming in second, and the husband, who appeared to have not missed too many large and fatty meals, came in a distant third. Storm knew if he didn't slow down, he would lose the humans, and the husband would have a heart attack.

The house they were heading for was only about six blocks away, Storm knew he could be there in about two minutes, but with the humans trailing behind, it took almost seven. At one point, he had slowed down enough that the police officer got to within about three feet of him, with the wife, still in second place but losing ground, trailing by about another four feet, and the husband, in the show position, turning a strange shade of purple, falling well behind. He picked up the pace enough to not get caught, but still close enough that they didn't lose him.

As he rounded the last corner and came within a few houses of where they were heading, he saw that the owners of the house had arrived back home and were heading to the front door. He let out a laugh as a new plan popped into his head, and off to his right hand side, he heard CB laugh as he quickly figured out what Storm had in mind. For an old cat, who claims to be too slow for this kind of game, CB seemed awfully spry as he trotted along beside the racing group.

"I thought you said you were old and out of shape." Storm yelled over at CB, with a laugh in his voice.

"Yeah, well, maybe not as out of shape as I let on." CB yelled back, "I love your new plan, let's hope the timing is right."

"Oh, it will be, just watch." Storm laughed.

As the fence surrounding the house came to within four feet, the race was over. Storm had won (with CB keeping an even pace with him), the police officer had come in second, the wife in third, and the husband, huffing and holding his chest, a very distant fourth. The second police officer, in the car, pulled up behind them at almost the exact same time.

***

Looking over the situation quickly, Storm saw that Keiko was on the far side of the yard, looking a bit stunned at the situation playing out in front of her. The humans who owned the house had just reached the front door and were placing the key in the lock. His race partners were close behind and CB, for some odd reason, was heading around to the far side of the yard, toward where Keiko was standing. He saw Keiko start to move, hesitantly, toward the group at the door and the front gate, then stopped and lay down.

"Now!", Storm said to himself, and with a leap he cleared the gate and ran at full speed toward the front door, diamond collar dangling from his teeth. Just as the male human turned the door handle and pushed the door open, with his and his wife's backs turned toward him, Storm slid past them, completely unnoticed.

Inside the house, he ran down the hallway, slid around the corner on the slick wooden floors, slammed into the far wall, regained his footing and scrambled down the hall to the bedroom Paradise was in. Dropping the collar at the door to her cage, he ran and leaped behind the overstuffed chair in the corner and hid from view.

***

At the same time that Storm slid past the humans at the front door, the police officer yelled at them. They turned around and saw the group gathered at the gate, but never saw the black cat run past them.

A conversation, punctuated with a significant amount of yelling and swearing ensued. It was obvious that the police, and Paradise's humans were accusing, and the owners of the house were denying.

This went on for several seconds, before everyone stopped in an odd silence, and listened. From inside the house they began to hear a low mewing. The sound gradually grew in intensity until it became the sound of a cat in distress. A low, sad, aching sound, strangely punctuated with what sounded like a cat laughing.

In seconds, Paradise's humans recognized the voice of their cat, but were confused by what sounded like a second cat, laughing. They prodded the police officer nearest them and quickly explained the situation. That was all the police needed to hear, and they forced entrance to the house. They followed the sound to the back bedroom, and just as they entered, the same small black cat they had been chasing ran out between their legs and disappeared out the front door. They could swear the cat was laughing.

In the center of the room they found a cage, a diamond collar, and the Grand Champion show cat. Arrests were immediately made, the cat was set free and given back to her humans, and a bunch of questions were asked of the husband of Paradise's owner as to whether he needed an ambulance, as he really didn't look very good.

***

From his spot behind the chair, Storm heard the commotion going on at the front door. He knew he had to get the humans inside, especially the police. He peeked his head around the corner of the chair and called out Paradise's name to catch her attention.

"Yeah, Storm?" Paradise replied.

"We need to get their attention, can you help out?" he asked earnestly.

"Storm, you have a lot to learn, I'm a show cat!! Getting people's attention is what I was bred to do. Watch and learn, young man." and with that, Paradise began a soft, low mewing which gradually grew in strength and intensity. This, Storm thought, would get anyone's attention.

Watching Paradise's performance, he was initially stunned at the production, then he found he could do nothing but laugh. There's a reason she's the worlds top show cat, he laughed to himself.

Out at the front door, he heard silence. Then in a burst of activity he heard voices rising, and people being pushed aside. He knew the humans were on their way. Looking over at Paradise, he said with a chuckle, "That was brilliant. It was a great pleasure meeting you. Unfortunately, it's about to get crazy in here, and I can't hang around for that. Good luck."

"Good luck to you, too, Storm. If there is ever any way I can return the favor, just let me know." Paradise replied.

"Will do." as he said this, the humans reached the door of the bedroom, and Storm bolted out from his hiding

place and ran, as fast as he could, through the tangle of
legs, around the corner, down the hall and out the front
door. All the while laughing like he had never laughed
before. He could not remember ever having so much fun.

Eight

CB slowed as he rounded the side of the yard. He had known Keiko for as long as he could remember, and had never seen her look as dejected as she did then. She lay in the corner of the yard, in the shade of a small tree, with her legs stretched out in front of her, and her giant head resting on her legs.

"Are you okay, Keiko?" CB said softly, "I've never seen you not respond when your humans were in trouble, before."

Keiko glanced at CB out of the corner of her eye, without even bothering to move her head, "I'm tired, CB. Well, maybe sick and tired is what should say." Keiko said quietly, her small, brown, bear-like eyes moist with frustration, "I'm just a dog who likes to work, and play and try to do something useful, and all I ever manage to do, is get hooked up with the worst kinds of humans imaginable. Why is that, CB? What is it about me that keeps leading me to this kind of situation? I really thought these people were better."

"You know, Keiko, this is going to sound like a platitude, and I really am sorry for that, but the reality is, it isn't you that's the problem. You are exactly what you say you are. Just a working dog, who wants a job to do. Unfortunately, you are a gigantic, strong working dog. People who do bad things want a dog like you, you scare people." CB paused to let this sink in. Keiko was at a turning point, she just needed to ask for help.

"CB, I don't want to do this anymore. I want a nice life, with a good human, who can love me for who I am, not for what I can be used for. Why is it that you run around helping every animal in the city, but won't help me?" Keiko asked, as a tear rolled down her giant cheek.

"Because, Keiko, I help animals who ask for help. You have never asked, or even really expressed a desire, for help. You needed to see the need for change for yourself, I couldn't force it on you. If, however, you are asking now, then I have never been more glad to have an animal ask for help from me in all my life, than I am right now." CB said with a smile. He had waited for years for this conversation.

"Yeah, I guess you have a point. But what can we do now? I'm stuck inside a fence, with yet another set of police officers getting ready to take me away and start the whole game over again." Keiko said with frustration.

"You're kidding me, right?" CB said with a chuckle, "You are the biggest dog I know, possibly the biggest animal I have ever known. Are you seriously telling me that a three foot wooden fence is going to stop you from getting out of that yard?"

"Ummm... what?" Keiko said in confusion.

"Keiko, for goodness sake... jump over the fence... or if that doesn't work, knock the fence over!!!" CB laughed.

"Oh, hey, that's a good idea." Keiko said, and the two old friends burst out laughing.

"Yeah, I kind of thought so. Come on, let's get out of here before anyone realizes what's going on OUTSIDE that house."

Keiko jumped up from her spot, looked over at the small, fragile fence, took a running leap and cleared it by at least a foot. Landing on the other side, she looked over at

CB and said, "Well, I guess it's time to start a new life. What do you have in mind?"

"I know the perfect place for you, you're gonna love this. It is a bit of a walk, though, about a mile, you up for that?" CB laughed.

"CB, I'm about ten times your size, you need at least four steps to equal one of mine. I think I can keep up." at this, the two old friends strolled off down the street, laughing at their new adventure.

***

The house CB led them to was about a mile from where CB's alley was located, in a pretty little, well kept neighborhood on the edge of The Heights. Jaffa, Ginka and Marti's apartments were just three blocks away.

"What are we doing here?" Keiko asked, as they stopped across the street from a large side-by-side duplex. The house sat on a lot of land slightly larger than their neighbors, and had an open field to the right of it. Plenty of space for a large dog to roam, though there was no fence, they could see a leash attached to the tree in front of the house. No worries, CB thought, Keiko will get used to a leash.

"Do you like this place, Keiko?" CB asked, all touch of humor gone from his voice. This was serious time now, if this didn't work, he wasn't sure what the next plan would be. Keiko couldn't live in the alley with he and Storm and the gang.

From the home on the right hand side of the duplex, two teenage kids emerged, a boy and his younger sister. They were laughing and joking with each other, and generally quite loud. CB glanced over at Keiko and saw the big dog smile. "Good." CB thought, she likes kids, hurdle number one taken care of.

As the parents followed the kids out of the house, into their car and out of the driveway, Keiko turned to CB.

"They look nice, who are they?" Keiko asked.

"Just some... well... let's just say they are old acquaintances of someone I used to know." CB replied enigmatically.

"Is this where you think I will fit in? I really like kids." Keiko said. CB could hear the excitement rising in her voice. Excellent, he thought, hurdle number two, she's getting excited.

"Well, yes and no. Actually, I am thinking of that person." CB said, and he and Keiko watched as a car pulled into the driveway of the home on the left side of the duplex. From the car stepped a tall woman with her long brown hair tied back and hanging almost all the way down her back. She had a kind, round face and was rubbing her eyes after a long day at work.

CB looked over at Keiko and saw the big dog almost melt. If ever there was such a think as love at first site, he had just witnessed it.

"Oh... CB... who is she? She looks so nice." Keiko asked quietly.

"She also is an old friend of someone I used to know. Can't say what her name is, you know how hard that human language is to understand." CB said.

"She looks kind of sad, does she like dogs?" Keiko asked.

"Oh, boy, does she! In fact, she particularly likes Akitas. That's why I brought you here. She has had several Akitas in her life, and the reason she looks sad, is that she recently lost her last one due to illness. She's an Akita lover, in need of an Akita. Do you think you can fit the bill?"

"You bet I can. She's not another master criminal, is she? I really don't want to deal with that again." Keiko asked.

CB burst out laughing, "No, Keiko." he said when he stopped laughing, "She is not a criminal mastermind. She's just a nice lady who loves Akitas. Do you want to meet her?"

"Yeah, I do. But she'll be afraid if I run over there." Keiko said with concern in her voice.

"Well, then, don't run. Take it slowly, and see what happens." CB advised, "Good luck, Keiko, I'll keep in touch to see how things go." but CB already knew how this would work out.

"Thanks, CB, I owe you." and with that, Keiko strolled across the street.

***

From his position across the street, CB watched as Keiko walked slowly toward the woman at the duplex. With a low chuff, Keiko caught the woman's attention. He saw the woman look around apprehensively at first, then down at the giant dog in front of her. What little concern the woman had melted immediately as she looked at the big dog who was now lowering her head, and looking up at her with the most beautiful, small, brown bear-like eyes she had ever seen.

Even from his perch across the street, CB could see the two new acquaintances immediately fall in love with each other. The woman reached out her hand, palm down, and the big dog raised her head to meet it. Slowly, the woman began rubbing the giant head, and small tulip shaped ears, and CB knew his work here was done.

With a smile, he turned and headed back to the alley.

The Cat Burglar
Inferno

One

"FIRE!!!"

That one word, screamed by a small, black and white cat named Max, was all it took to set the entire alley into motion. CB and Storm, who had been in the middle of the same conversation Storm had been pushing since they first met; the question of who CB's former human was, what CB's real name is and why he didn't use that name, jumped up from their respective seats and began running down the alley. They ran into Max about halfway down the alley.

"What fire, where?" CB yelled to Max as they ran towards him.

Max skidded to a halt in front of CB and Storm, "It, ummm..." Max said hesitantly, "CB, it's at the animal shelter."

Storm felt the blood turn to ice in his veins as he heard this. Beside him, CB replied, "Oh, no!" with the saddest note he had ever heard from the old cat.

"CB, wait, won't the human fire department take care of this?" Storm said hopefully.

"The fire department is volunteer. Most of the members don't live in town, and have to drive to get here. Also, it's three o'clock in the morning, unless the fire is raging, no one will notice and call them." CB said as they ran.

"Don't they have an alarm?"

"It doesn't work" CB replied.

"How do you know?" Storm yelled as they reached the other cats at the head of the alley.

"I used to live there!" CB said.

Storm stopped dead in is tracks and stared at the old cat. He what? Surely he had heard wrong, but this was no time to chat. He heard CB start to give instructions.

"Max... go get Jaffa, Ginka and Marti. Norton... find Rocky and Herbie. Storm... go get Keiko. The rest of you follow me... we'll all meet at the shelter. NOW! GO!!" as they continued to run out into the street and turn toward the shelter, Storm yelled over his shoulder, "CB, how long will it take for the fire department to get there."

"Best case? At least fifteen minutes after they find out there IS a fire." CB yelled.

Storm felt a chill run through him, "CB, they'll all be dead by then." he said softly.

"That's why we need to hurry. Go get Keiko, we can't do this without her."

And with that, the two friends separated and ran as fast as they could. CB to the shelter and Storm to go find the biggest dog in the city.

Two

Storm shuddered with frustration when he reached the duplex which Keiko now called her home. The large, two story brick building was completely dark, "Of course it is," he said to himself with frustration welling up inside him, "it's three o'clock in the darned morning!"

Running the situation through his head as quickly as he could, he decided to throw caution to the wind, and screamed Keiko's name as loud as he could.

He got nothing in reply. No response, whatsoever, "Of course," he said quickly to himself, "I really didn't know what I expected that was going to accomplish."

So, he yelled again. And again, and again and again, until he saw a light come on in one of the upstairs windows. Seconds later that light was followed by a light on the lower level, and finally he saw the back door open, and Keiko's human reach out and grab the leash hanging on the wall. Another few seconds, and Keiko was running across the lawn toward him.

"Storm, for goodness sake, what's wrong?" Keiko said as she ran.

"Fire."

"Oh, no. Where?" Keiko said with her heart in her throat.

"The animal shelter." Storm replied.

"NO!!" Keiko yelled, and with a burst of energy she started running along with Storm. She had run about ten feet when the length of her leash ran out. Her head whipped around as she was yanked off her feet, and went sprawling across the lawn.

"Storm, help. The rope is nylon. It's too strong for me to break."

Storm turned around and ran back to the giant dog, "Keep your head down, and keep the rope tight." he said as he ran. In a second he was back to the dog, and began chewing on the rope. Another few seconds and he had chewed through the rope, which separated with a loud twang.

Again the two began running. Storm did a quick calculation in his head. Two and a half minutes to get from the alley to Keiko's house, another minute and a half to get Keiko outside and freed from the leash, and it would take another two or three minutes to get to the shelter. A total of six or seven minutes. Time was wasting away.

"Come on, Keiko, we need to hurry." he yelled. And with renewed effort the two friends hurtled toward the shelter.

Three

CB was the first to arrive at the shelter. It was a small, brick building with windows across the front, that stood only a single story high. There was a parking lot in the front and along the left side, and a loading dock around the back. On the right hand side was an open field where the animals, well really just the dogs, could be taken for a walk.

CB, without hesitation, ran to the back of the building. The loading dock was little more than a large concrete slab where cars and trucks could park to load, or more commonly unload, the food, crates and supplies necessary to run the shelter. In the center of the building, by the dock, was a wooden door with an upper and lower panel and a solid cross beam in the center. Looking at the door, CB was glad to see they had not replaced it with a more sturdy one.

He saw smoke seeping out from under under the door, but it was still minimal, he had seen slightly more coming out from under the front door and the windows, but no flames. It was a dark and overcast night, there was no way the humans would notice this yet. CB heard a low, frustrated growl and looked around him, only to realize he was still alone, and it was he who was making the sound. "Calm yourself, old man." he said to himself, "You can't help anyone if you lose control yourself."

Just as he finished his self chastisement, the other cats began arriving. First came the team from the alley. All strong and smart cats, but definitely the workers, not the leaders. Then came Max with Jaffa, Ginka and Marti, followed closely by Norton with Rocky and Herbie. Finally, his leaders had arrived.

He was just starting to turn and begin giving his instructions, when out of the corner of his eye he saw, at the top of the hill three blocks away, a gigantic black and white dog, and a small black cat hurtling toward the shelter, and his heart leapt. Keiko and Storm had arrived, there was a chance this might work. He was amazed at the speed with which they had arrived, he had not expected them for another couple minutes.

"Listen up everyone." CB yelled, "I want you to set yourselves up in the field to the right. Keep some distance between you, it's going to get crazy, and we don't need different groups feeding off each other emotionally." he stopped for a second, then continued.

"I'm going to separate you all into groups, stake out a spot in the field as I call your names. Ginka and Marti, you're in charge of kittens. Jaffa and Norton, puppies. Rocky and Herbie, adult cats. Max, the small animals, rabbits, hamsters, gerbils that type of thing if there are any. Keiko will take care of the adult dogs. Storm will keep everything organized and I will go in and get whoever I can, out." he looked around at the rest of the cats from the alley, "The rest of you, set up a perimeter, we need to watch for humans. We need to see them when they arrive, and we have to make sure they don't see us being this organized, it would just confuse them to see that we can work together. Also, I want some of you to act as runners. As I get the animals out, I want some of you to guide them to the proper area in the field."

Again CB stopped, he felt like he was missing something, but he was sure he wasn't. It was at that second that Storm and Keiko finally arrived, shaking and out of breath, "Sorry." Storm huffed, "We got here as fast as we could." he said while trying to catch his breath.

"No problem, I'm stunned you made it this quick." CB replied.

"Yeah, well... that dog has some seriously long legs, I almost had trouble keeping up with her." Storm gasped, "So, what's the plan?"

"I set the teams up in the field, different animals to different groups. Storm, you will take over coordination. Keiko, after you help me get in, you will take care of any adult dogs." CB said quickly.

"First things first." CB continued, "Keiko, the lower panel of that door is made of lighter wood than the frame or the cross beam. If you hit it just right, it will break and I can get in."

"Great idea." Storm said, "What's your plan?" he asked earnestly.

"Past the wooden door is an entryway, then a glass door. The glass door will be locked, from the inside, but there is a small window above it that is usually open. There's a table next to the door that I can use to get me up high enough to jump up to the window and crawl through. From there, I can unlock the door and pull it open. Once I, or rather, Keiko, pushes it far enough it will keep itself open. I am not big enough to push it that far. From there, I can open the cages and start getting the animals out." CB finished.

"Great plan. How do you get the cages open?" Storm asked.

"You lift the latches and pull them to the left. Why, what does that matter?" CB asked with some confusion in his voice, he needed to get moving.

"Well, it matters because there is no way you are going in there, and I need to know how to do it." Storm replied quietly.

"Storm, we don't have time for me to argue with you." CB said tersely.

"Good, then shut up and listen. I am smaller and thinner than you, and I can jump higher. I can get through that window easier than you can. Also, once these animals are out here, they know you better, they will listen to you faster than they will me. You need to run the show, not me. I'll get in, get the cages open, get the animals out to you, and you make sure everything runs smoothly." Storm said forcefully. CB started to argue, then realized Storm was right.

"Fine. Agreed. You know it drives me crazy when you're right." CB chuckled.

"Alright, well, that was easier than I expected." Storm said a bit sheepishly, "Let's go, we're wasting time. Keiko, get that door open." Storm said.

"Got it." Keiko replied. Turning quickly she started off toward the door.

Four

It was a little over twenty five feet from where they were standing to where the door was. Plenty of room for Keiko to get up to full speed. She kept herself low, and her head down and covered the distance in a matter of seconds. As she ran she looked closely at the door. The top and bottom panels were definitely the key spots, "But!" she thought. About two and a half feet from the door she changed her plan and, keeping her head tucked down and turned to the left, she leapt with all her strength.

Keiko's shoulder hit the small wooden door squarely in the middle of the center cross beam, and the door exploded. She had noticed as she ran that the door was old and dry. She could expect it to be brittle. Heck, she thought, every human she had lived with up to the last one, had let their houses fall apart, she could recognize a worn out wooden door better than any animal in town. Or any human for that matter.

As the weight of her body carried her across the entryway, she slammed into the glass door which CB had described earlier, and the entire building shook from the impact. As she stood up from her crumbled position at the foot of the glass door and looked through the glass, her breath left her in a giant gasp. Beyond the door, the shelter was bathed in rippling orange flames.

As fast as she could, she scrambled to her feet and ran back out of the building.

***

CB and Storm, and the rest of the cats in the area watched in stunned disbelief as Keiko not only opened the door for them, but completely destroyed it. They had the entire opening to work with, rather than the small opening they were expecting. Quickly a cheer rose from the assembled cats.

It was then, as CB and Storm joined in the cheer, that they looked past Keiko and simultaneously let out a gasp. The inside of the shelter, they could see clearly, was engulfed in flames. Storm started running toward the building and CB held him back.

"No, Storm, stop. It's too far gone." CB said as he watched Keiko come running back out of the building.

"I have to CB, those animals will die if we don't help." Storm yelled.

"You'll die if you go in there." CB countered, "Let me go, I'm older, and more expendable."

"You're also an idiot, I stand a better chance, let go of me." Storm screamed, and with the strength and skill he had learned from lifetime of fighting to get what he needed, he struck out at CB, and pushed the older cat away. Now free, and knowing it would only be for a second before the older, stronger and wiser cat subdued him again, he ran for the door.

CB reached out for him as he ran, but missed him by a hair. Storm, with all his youthful speed got past him and headed for the door. About halfway there he passed Keiko heading the opposite direction.

"Stop, you fool. You can't survive in there." Keiko yelled at him. But Storm rushed past him, responding only with, "Neither will they, Keiko. Just get that door held open once I get it unlocked."

Five

Storm crossed over the threshold that had once contained a wooden door, and now only contained splinters. He saw the table CB had mentioned and jumped up on it. It was a solid, iron table with a granite top, but he didn't notice any of that. As soon as his feet touched the table, he spun to his left and looked above the glass door. There, just as CB had said, was a small window being held open by a metal bar.

Without thinking, he shifted his body weight and launched himself toward the window. His head cleared the opening, and his front paws, and he immediately lifted his hind legs and caught his claws on the window sill. With one great push from his powerful hind legs, he was through the window and falling toward the floor.

As he landed, he spun around and faced the door. The heat in the room was terrifying, and he could feel his whiskers bristle as he looked at the lock in the door. As a former burglar, he had seen countless doors with an endless variety of locking mechanisms. He knew this one well, and for him, it was one of the worst. A small latch about an inch across and a quarter of an inch wide, that had to be turned to remove the bolt from the door frame.

Without thinking he rushed the door, reached up with his paws, and putting one on each side of the knob, he started trying to turn it. He was vaguely aware of the heat of the latch, but he didn't care about that. All that concerned him was getting it turned. He struggled, and struggled and finally, with a screech of effort, felt it turn. A sharp clunk as the bolt released was music to his ears.

From beyond the glass door, he could see Keiko standing in the entryway, waiting for him to succeed. When the latch finally turned, Keiko hit the door with her full weight. The door shot open, and she continued pushing until she felt it catch and stay open.

"Thanks, Keiko. Now go back and tell CB to get ready for some guests." Storm said.

"Are you okay, Storm." Keiko asked quickly.

"I'm great, go." Storm said, even as he felt the pads of his front paws start to ache from the burn they had received at the lock, "I'll worry about that later," he thought, "too much to do now." and he turned and started running down the hallway.

***

CB watched vacantly as Storm rushed past him and into the burning building. He admired the bravery, but knew there was no hope here. He instinctively started running to help his friend, when he was stopped short by the giant Akita.

"Now, now, CB, as the old saying goes, let's not throw effort after foolishness." Keiko said as she held CB in place, "He seems to know what he's doing. Let him do it, or die trying."

CB stopped fighting, looked around him and stopped. Storm and Keiko had their work to do, but so did he. With a sigh, he told the big dog to get off of him and turned to his team, "Fine." he said, "If Storm succeeds... when Storm succeeds... we will have some very sick animals coming out. Everyone get ready." and with that he turned back to watch the door, fear for his friend weighing heavy on his heart.

Six

Storm looked down the hallway and was stunned by his luck. The majority of the fire was on the left side of the building, and the majority of the animals were on the right. But, what to do. Should he release the animals in the most danger, those in the fire, or those who have the better chance at survival. With no time to ponder it, he made a rash decision.

Turning to the right, he ran to the nearest cage, lifted the latch and pushed it. Inside, two small kittens huddled in the corner, "Come on, you two, no time to dawdle. Run out past the glass door and outside, there is a team out there to help you. Go, go, go." he said as the little kittens ran down the hallway.

As quickly as possible he continued down the hall releasing the animals as he went. There was no rhyme or reason to the sorting of the animals. He had expected dogs in one section, cats in another. But, there was no reasonable sorting. With a chuckle he realized he was being an idiot. Here he was, trying desperately to save the animals, and all he was thinking about was the random nature of their placement within the cages.

Finally, he reached the end of the hallway and found several bird cages. Under normal circumstances, a small bird would have been a snack. Now, it was just another life, desperate to escape. As quickly as possible, he jumped onto a shelf where he was able to reach the cages and, instead of messing around with the latches, he simply knocked them over and, as they hit the floor, they broke open. The birds flew down the hall and out the door.

Then, he turned to the other side of the building. The heat was becoming oppressive, and he was having more and more trouble breathing. He was getting light headed. Crouching as close to the floor as he could, he found a pocket of fresh air and took a deep fill of it into his lungs. Then, with the energy he found in the fresh oxygen, he ran across the hall and into the flames.

***

The heat, as he crossed to the other side of the shelter knocked Storm off his feet. He lay in a huddle on the floor of the shelter trying to catch his breath. He could see seven cages on this side of the shelter. All of them had animals in them.

Panting, and trying with every fiber of his being, he pulled himself up and headed for the nearest cage. Inside was a small, female black lab he knew immediately. "Maggie." he croaked, "What are you doing in here?"

"Please, Storm. Help me." Maggie said, "My humans lost me when I chased after a rabbit and left the yard."

Storm summoned his strength and reached up to unlatch the cage, his eyes blurring, and his breathing shallow. Slowly, he reached the latch and slid it open. The scared little dog rushed past him and headed toward the front door. Moving as fast as he could, he reached the next cage and found it empty. He was losing touch with what was going on.

Still, he kept going. With all his effort focused, he tried to move on to the next cage. But, as he moved, the smoke in his lungs, nose and eyes overcame him and he collapsed. He knew he was losing the battle with the smoke and heat, but still kept trying to move. It was all in vain, and he collapsed.

As he hit the floor, and consciousness began to slip away, he could swear he saw a blur of black and white rush past him, then the world went black and he could no longer breath.

Seven

Out in the parking lot, CB saw a parade of animals begin rushing out the shattered door. The first were some kittens, "Get them over to the field, and make sure Ginka knows they might have inhaled some smoke and could have some trouble breathing."

Step by step, the animals exited the shelter and were guided to the appropriate section of the field. He saw Marti telling stories to the kittens to keep them calm as Ginka checked them over for injury. He looked further and saw Norton running around entertaining the puppies like the nut he is. CB laughed for a second, watching the scene.

Further on, he saw Rocky and Herbie telling stories to the older cats. Only Max was still waiting for animals to entertain. But, then, the animals coming to him had very short legs, it could take a while.

Keiko, meanwhile had checked over the older dogs, and made sure their wounds were addressed. Overall, everything was going fairly well. He was giving some orders to one of his cats when one of the others let out a yelp. CB ran over to where the cat was keeping watch and saw what everyone was hoping for. The human fire department was only about four blocks away.

"Everyone listen up. The humans are almost here. When they pull into the parking lot, get out. Those of you who were in the shelter, please wait. The humans will make sure you are safe and well cared for. Please do not follow us, we can't afford to get caught." he said, realizing how harsh it may have sounded. But these animals needed care, and his team needed to get away.

As he turned back to the shelter, he saw three small birds fly past, followed by a small black lab.

"Maggie, what are you doing here?" CB said as he ran toward the little dog.

Coughing and spitting, and with her eyes watering from the smoke, Maggie managed to choke out, "Got away from house, chasing rabbit."

"Where's Storm?" he asked anxiously.

"Don't know." she coughed.

As he was trying to help her across the parking lot, and wondering how much longer Storm would need, Keiko suddenly blew past him heading toward the small building.

"Keiko, stop. Where are you going?" CB yelled as Keiko ran past.

"He's in trouble, CB, I need to get him." Keiko replied.

"I'll take care of getting him, you take care of Maggie." CB yelled.

"No, if Storm is hurt, you aren't big enough to get him out. I am. Get the rest of the team out of here and back to the alley before the humans get here." Keiko yelled as she ran, and then she was lost in the smoke as she ran into the burning building.

***

The heat hit Keiko like a brick wall as she entered the smoldering building. Instantly, she gasped for breath and felt the burning smoke tear at her throat. With her eyes watering, she stopped to cough, in hopes of getting some of the smoke out of her lungs. She succeeded, to some extent, only to have it all replaced with the next breath. Frustration began to rise in her. Suddenly, she wasn't sure what to do.

It was too dark in the building, and there was too much smoke, for her to be able to see. Somewhere in this mess was a cat she was certain was in trouble. In a desperate attempt, she tried to yell out Storm's name, but her throat was too clogged with smoke for sound to come out.

Looking around her, she saw a series of cages on the right which were all empty, and recognized a climbing tower for cats. The kittens came out first, she thought. Storm started on this side. That means he ended over there. And with that she turned her head to the left, and shuddered. That entire side of the building was a ball of flames.

As quickly as she could she moved as far to the left as she possible, and began moving down the hallway. Her way was blocked by the remains of broken cages, and the smoke in her eyes made vision almost impossible. She tried yelling again, but it was a waste of breath.

Still she moved on, further and further down the hall. Frustration continued to rise in her as the inability to see and breathe hindered her attempts. And, she realized, as the oxygen decreased, so did her ability to think. She was losing her way. In desperation, she growled her frustration.

In reply, she heard a movement in front of her. Not the roaring movement of the fire, or the metallic movement of the collapsing cages, but a softer movement. An animal.

Rushing forward, she saw Storm slide slowly to the ground, as his consciousness left him. Quickly, she nudged him with her nose, and got no response. She placed her ear to his chest, but there was so much noise she couldn't hear anything. Taking a last breath, as deep as she could, she reached down and clamped her teeth on the scruff of Storm's neck, picked him up, turned and ran as fast as she could toward the exit of the building. Hoping, beyond all hope, that she wasn't too late.

Eight

Back in the alley, life was anything but back to
normal. The majority of the cats had returned to their
usual homes, but their thoughts all ran to the same topic.
Storm. That, they all agreed, was one very sick cat.

CB sat in his chair in the entryway that he and
Storm called home. In the far corner, Jaffa and Marti were
curled together talking quietly, and in front of him, on the
pillow he had made his own, lay Storm. It had only been
thirty minutes since Max had alerted them to the fire, and
ten since Keiko had dropped Storm on his pillow before
returning to her home, and still Storm had not regained
consciousness. Twenty minutes was all it had taken from
the time they learned of the fire, to the time they were back
home. CB was stunned by that, it had seemed like hours.

The burns on Storm's front paws and left ear had
been cleaned and wrapped in strips from a clean white
cloth which CB had laying around for whenever injuries
occurred. And currently, Ginka was sitting next to Storm,
gingerly cleaning the soot out of the fur around his eyes.

CB took a moment to look carefully at the four cats
in front of him. Ginka and Storm, Jaffa and Marti. Pretty
good matches, those were. Not that he considered
matchmaking part of his job, but it had worked this time.

As he watched, Storm slowly moved his head in
response to the grooming he was receiving, "Good." CB
said aloud, "It looks like our old friend is finally coming
around."

Ginka stopped her grooming and looked at Storm
closely. He looked like he had been in a car wreck. Fur

was missing all over him, and his front paws would take days to heal. He had been amazingly brave and she could not be more proud of him.

Slowly, Storm opened his eyes and looked around as if he was not sure where he was. Then, with a jump he tried to get up as he yelled, "CB, the animals, we have to get them out."

***

Storm's mind was floating somewhere off in space. He couldn't remember much, only that he had been trying to do something, he couldn't remember what, to help someone, but he couldn't remember who. He could feel a light brushing motion around his eyes and found it enjoyable. He moved toward the feeling, and slowly opened his eyes.

Suddenly, the whole world came back to him and he jumped. Pain flashed through his entire body, and his paws felt like they were on fire. But he remembered it all now, he struggled to get up but CB and Ginka had him held down, "CB, the animals, we have to get them out." he yelled.

"Storm, stop. We're all done with the animals. You're going to hurt yourself... well, worse than you already are." CB said quickly.

"Did they all get out?" Storm said anxiously, his voice rising.

"Yeah, Storm, most of them did." CB said honestly.

"Most? How many didn't make it, CB." Storm asked as he struggled again to get up.

"We think there were five that didn't make it out, Storm. You really did an amazing job in there." the pride in CB's voice was so thick it could be cut with a knife.

Storm absorbed this information with sadness. He tried to respond but his voice cracked and a tear rolled down his cheek, "I tried, CB, I really did. I'm so sorry we didn't get them all." he said quietly.

"Storm," CB said softly, "I really wasn't sure we would be able to help ANY of them. It was a long shot at best. I have never been more proud of any animal in my life as I am of you right now." CB said.

Storm sat silently for a moment thinking this through. He was frustrated and felt he had failed, yet there was a lot to be said for what CB had said. If they hadn't done what they did, all of the animals would be dead.

"Where's Keiko? Is she okay? I could swear I saw her just as the smoke overtook me." Storm asked.

"She went back home. She didn't want to scare her human any more than she had. She was gone almost twenty minutes, her human would have been getting very worried and would have been out looking for her. And, you are right, Keiko was the one who found you and pulled you from the fire. Without her, you would probably be dead now." CB replied.

"I'll need to go talk to her."

"Yeah, but it can wait. You have some healing to do. Your paws and ear are in pretty bad shape, but they should heal just fine, it looks fairly superficial. Rest up for a couple days and we'll see if your nurse allows you to wander." CB chuckled.

Storm looked over at Ginka and felt his heart go out to the young cat, "That would be you, I imagine." he said.

"Yep, and I say you stay." she said with a laugh.

"Is this what I can expect from dating you?" Storm asked.

"Who says we're dating?" Ginka laughed.

"Who says we aren't?" Storm replied and the two started laughing with each other.

"He'll be fine, CB." Ginka said and slapped Storm on his shoulder.

Nine

When the laughter finally died down, and word was spread throughout the alley that Storm would probably be fine in a few days, the five friends got to chatting.

"So," CB said with a smile, "It looks like we have some dating going on around here."

"Yeah, looks like it. So... that leaves you as the old bachelor in the group." Storm said, "What are we going to do about that?"

"YOU... are not going to do anything about it. As it turns out, I also am working on that issue, myself." CB said.

"Really?" the group all yelled in unison.

"Yeah... you all remember Paradise, I'm sure. Well, she and I are trying to rekindle an old flame. Just a couple problems, of course. She can't come to the alley, and I can't hang out in her mansion... her humans would not approve. We're... well, we're working on it." CB said with a laugh and a shake of his head.

"Oh, no, not again." Storm said with a sigh and a roll of his eyes, "You do this all the time. You drop hints about your past, then refuse to give details. Like that bombshell about having lived in the shelter. Enough, fill us in. Who are you?"

CB looked over at his closest friends and sighed. Maybe it was time. Maybe the past needed to become the past, and not something he ran from.

"You never give up, do you, Storm?" he said.

"Nope, never." Storm replied.

"This is what you are going to have to live with, you know." he said to Ginka.

"Well, not all the time. He lives in the alley and I live a few blocks away with some wonderful humans. Looks like we have the same issue you and Paradise have. Except, of course, I get to be out of the house whenever I want, unlike Paradise. We'll... work it out." she said looking over at Storm, "But, your delaying. Tell us the story."

"Fine!" CB said quietly. This was new territory, this level of trust, but he knew it was right, "To begin with..." he began softly, "My name... is Tyler. I'm eleven years old."

For a moment he paused and looked over the group. They were staring at him with all their attention directed at him, and soft smiles on their faces. His friends, he thought. I can trust them. Leaning back in his chair he cleared his throat.

"I was born on a small farm about eight miles outside of town. It wasn't a big place, but they grew enough to feed their family, and some left over to sell to make some money. They also had a few cows, some chickens, and this crazy old dog, who must have been a thousand years old." CB laughed at the memory, he hadn't thought about that crazy old dog in years, "I am quite certain he was senile, but if not, he certainly didn't have all his neurons firing at the same time. The farmer constantly had to keep him from chasing the mean old bull in the pasture.

"Anyway, I was the last born of a litter of five, and I... well, I had some issues. I was the smallest of the five, by far, and I wasn't big enough to fight my way over for food. I know, that sounds incredible now... I did fill out well in the end." again he stopped and laughed with his friends.

"The farmer was an incredibly kind man. He noticed me in the litter and that I wasn't getting any milk, and he did the unexpected. You see, he was a farmer. Animals, to him, were a commodity, or a tool. Cows gave milk, chicken gave eggs and made a good dinner, dogs kept the place safe, and cats... well, cats kept rats away. A scrawny, underfed kit was usually either left to die, or was taken away and destroyed. But, something odd came together when I was born. You see, the old farmer's wife had passed away a few months before I was born, and the old man had this big hole in his heart. I don't think he actually thought I would become a companion of his, farmers don't have companion animals, I think he just figured he would get me healthy and send me back to the barn.

"The problem is, we just started growing on each other. He started feeding me with a dropper, then a spoon, a saucer, a cup and finally a bowl. Then came the first solid meats. This took months, and I grew well. And by the time I reached the point where he was ready to send me back to the barn, we were the best of friends.

"I slept at the foot of his bed, I curled up on his lap in the evenings, we played with toys and ate from the same plate. I wasn't a barn cat, I was his friend. He would open the door to me in the morning, and let me roam the farm. I would play with my family, run around the farm, even chase rats. But in the end, I was not a barn cat, I was a house cat. Every night, the door was opened and I went in to spend the evening with my human."

CB stopped and shook his head. He hadn't told anyone this story in years... in fact, he thought, it was Paradise he had last told the story to, and they hadn't dated in years. I'm getting old, he thought.

"We went on this way for four years. You have heard me say that there are great humans, good humans, and not so good humans. Well, he set the bar for great humans. He was kind, he was caring, he was even tempered and he had opened his heart to me and it was never going to be closed again.

"Then, one morning... I remember it was bitterly cold out, one of those really nasty winter days, where I had no plan of even considering going outside. Anyway, I woke up and noticed that he was still in bed. It was getting light and he had work to do, so I jumped on him, and meowed at him and he didn't move." CB stopped and wiped a tear from his eye. He was a good human, he thought with a broken heart.

"His son come over later in the day to pick up some equipment, and found him. He had died during the night. His son and his wife eventually sold the farm, but since his wife was allergic to me, and they didn't feel I could survive in the barn, I was a companion cat, after all, I was sent to the animal shelter." CB stopped and took a deep breath. This was every bit as hard as he thought it would be, but he was glad to be getting it out in the open. Letting out a sigh, he continued.

"You have all seen the animal shelter, some of you in more depth than you wanted, I'd wager. Well, the thing about the people who come to the shelter to adopt animals, is that they only want young animals. Kittens and puppies are the name of the game. They don't want a four year old cat. Especially one who is heartbroken, depressed and a bit surly... which is a great description of my attitude at the time.

"So, one night after being in the shelter for about a month, I noticed a few things. First, after watching the keepers for a while, I knew how the latch to my cage worked. Second, I saw the window above the glass door. And third, and most important, I saw that the last keeper out had not shut the wooden door completely, and it had not locked.

"I reached out of my cage, lifted the latch and pulled it. The door swung open. I talked to several of the other animals to see if they wanted to join me and only four cats agreed, all the other animals were too scared, too old or too ill to come along. Those four cats you know, by the way. They were Rocky, Herbie, Max and Norton. But, we wouldn't work together for a while.

"Getting out of the shelter was easy, surviving was the challenge. I was a house cat, I was not used to scrounging my own food. And, while I eventually learned, I did not like it. So, it occurred to me one day, that humans like shiny things. If I took them shiny things, they might feed me. And, the Cat Burglar was born.

"I was extremely good, if I do say so myself. This went on for a year or two, just kind of bouncing around, before I found one gentleman who had a particular liking for my talents. I stayed with him, he fed me, I stole for him, and life was pretty good. It was during this time that I met Paradise.

"Her humans were immensely wealthy by human standards, and I made regular trips to her house. She loved her humans, but couldn't care less about the shiny baubles. She did, however, like hanging out with one of the Bad Boys From Jones, as she called me. This went on for another couple years before the real problem set in.

"You see, my human at that time was not the worst human in the world, but he was gradually getting worse. You asked me once, Storm, why I recognized your potential and understood your situation so well. Well, it's because I had lived it.

"It all came to a head one day, when my human got angry with me because he didn't like the quality of the items I brought to him. He yelled and screamed, which I was used to, he even threw something, which I was also used to. But, when one of those things, a glass he was drinking from and threw, shattered and a piece of it cut my ear. Well, let's just say that 'he made me angry' is pretty much the understatement of the century.

"I had never been that mad, and for a second, I lost control. Okay, it was more than a second. You have to understand, by now, I was no longer the runt of the litter. I was a solid fifteen pound cat with four years of experience fighting off other animals to steal things from their humans. I was one tough cat. And I was furious. Without thinking, I threw myself at him and slashed him with my claws. Then, I just kept slashing. By the time I came to my senses, the man was in big trouble. I have never seen that much blood before, or since.

"I realized a lot of things coming out of that anger. I learned I needed to keep close control over my anger. I learned I was sick and tired of that life, much as Keiko decided a while ago, and I learned about the human police. That was the first time I needed to get the attention of the human police, so they could help me. My human needed an ambulance, and I couldn't call one.

"I ran to the local police station, caught their attention and led them to the house. They saved his life, but it was three weeks before he got out of the hospital. And then, it was to go to jail for all the stolen goods they found in his house.

"It was also then that I learned that there might be a way to help, rather than harm, people and other animals. And, that... is how I ended up here. The human police were looking for me, based upon the description my human had given them, so I had to hide. I found this alley, and Rocky, Herbie, Max and Norton, and started a new life.

"The rest, as they say, is history. Now, if you don't mind, I haven't talked this much, for this long, in years, I need some water." he jumped down and went over to the bowl they filled regularly with fresh water from a stream near by.

When he returned he saw the team looking at him with a mix of wonder and awe. Ginka broke the silence "That's quite a story. Thanks for telling us. I can see why you didn't want to tell it. Do you think the human police are still looking for you?"

"After all these years, I doubt it. But, I like my life here now, so I don't see any need for change." he said with a smile.

"I have a question." Storm said with a laugh, "Does this mean we can start calling you by a real name, rather than a title, now?"

"If you must, I guess I can't stop you." CB said, but everyone gathered knew that he would welcome hearing that name again. It would remind him of good times.

Ten

It took a week before Storm's paws had healed enough for him to walk all the way to where Keiko now lived. It was a sunny, warm day, and the birds chirped loudly in the trees as he enjoyed a leisurely stroll the few blocks it took to get to the duplex.

He passed children playing in the park, and young couples sharing a quiet lunch. Life, as he thought of it, could not have been better.

When he arrived at the house, he saw Keiko hooked to her leash in the back yard. A new leash, he noticed, but still nylon, he could chew through it again if needed, he chuckled to himself.

The big dog was laying comfortably with her legs out in front of her and her head resting on them. She could have been napping for all Storm knew, but, no... her eyes were open.

As Storm approached the giant dog, he didn't say a word, and neither did Keiko. Silently, he walked directly up to the big dog until they were face to face. He looked into the dogs small, brown bear-like eyes for a second, then leaned forward and put his forehead on hers and held it there. For a second the two friends closed their eyes and relished the moment.

"Thank you." Storm said so softly he hardly even heard it himself.

"Your welcome." the big dog replied.

The Cat Burglar:
Gentle Ben

One

"Tyler?" Storm said as he walked toward the entryway he shared with his best friend.

Tyler chuckled. He had been called CB for so long, it still seemed strange to hear his real name again. Yet, the name brought back some great memories, it was nice to hear.

"Tyler?" Storm repeated.

"What?" Tyler said.

"Who's Ben?" Storm asked.

"WHAT?" Tyler said as he jumped up and ran out to meet his friend.

"I said, who's Ben?" Storm repeated.

"I heard what you said. Why are you asking it?" Tyler said with frustration.

"Oh, sorry. He's out at the entry to the alley, and is asking for you." Storm replied.

"Well, go get him, will you?" Tyler asked.

"Sure, who is he?" Storm asked.

"He's my brother." Tyler said.

"Really? Cool." Storm replied, and headed back out to the alley entry.

***

Ben was a large cat, just like Tyler. With the same thick medium length fur, and a similar charcoal grey color. His chest was more white than Tyler's beige, and he had more black on his legs, but it was easy to see the family relation.

Storm chatted with him as they walked down the alley, and found him to be one of the kindest, and most pleasant cats he had ever met. There was a hint of Tyler's self control in him, but he was much more soft spoken, and seemed to smile more easily. Gentle was the word that jumped to Storm's mind.

Storm knew Tyler's history, and understood why he was so serious, but he also knew that Tyler's family members were raised differently from him. They were barn cats. He was a house cat. Yet, he knew that Tyler had always maintained a good relationship with his family.

He watched as Tyler and Ben butted heads in the time honored greeting of two cats who cared for each other.

"Ben." Tyler said with a smile, "It is so great to see you. Welcome to the alley, I can't believe how long it has been since you were here last." Tyler said.

"I know, it's just been rather crazy at the farm. We have loved your visits though." Ben said softly.

"How often do you get out to the farm, Tyler?" Storm asked.

"I try to get there every few weeks, but it has been a while now. What with the whole 'fire' thing." Tyler said with a chuckle.

"I heard about that and I must say, we are all very impressed. Not to mention how glad we are that Storm came out of it okay." Ben said earnestly.

"Thanks, it worked out much better than we expected." Tyler replied, "So, other than a chat, what brings you to the big city?" he asked.

"Well," Ben sad softly, "there's a problem out at the farm, and I could use another set of eyes, and another opinion on what to do. Could you take a run out there with me?"

"Sure, I'd love to. Things around here are pretty well controlled, you want to come with us Storm?" Tyler asked.

"Really? Yeah, that would be great. Jaffa can keep an eye on things, and I think Max and Norton are around." Storm replied.

"Great, let's go. I think you'll love the farm, Storm." Ben said.

"Well, it should be interesting, I've never seen a farm before." Storm replied.

"Really? Well, this should be a real treat, then. Let's go." Ben said.

After a quick word with Max to let him know what was going on, and to have him let Jaffa know he was in charge for a while, Storm, Tyler and Ben headed out of the alley and started the eight mile walk to the farm where Tyler grew up.

Two

Storm stood on the dirt driveway of the farm and looked slowly around him. This was the first time he had been on a farm, and was stunned. This was CB's home. No, wait, he goes by Tyler now, he chuckled, he was having fun reminding him of his name.

On his right was the farm house. It stood two stories high, had a porch that wrapped around two sides and was painted sunshine yellow, with white trim. This was where Tyler's human had taken him in when he was born and was too small and weak to live with his family in the barn. His human had fed him until he was strong enough to rejoin the family, but by that time he and his human were so closely bonded, that there was no way he could be a barn cat. He was a house cat... a companion to a lonely old man who had found joy in his life from a small grey cat.

Directly ahead of him was a gigantic red barn with white trim, and a small garage large enough to hold two cars. The barn, he knew, was where Ben, and the rest of Tyler's family, lived. He could see a small cat sitting by the door to the barn.

To the left, Storm saw a gigantic, open field, and in the distance, another farm.

"Holy smokes, CB, this is where you grew up? This is fantastic. Why did you ever leave. Oh, wait, sorry, I know why you left." Storm mumbled shyly.

"No problem, Storm. The past is the past, and it made me who who I am. And why am I suddenly CB again?" Tyler said with a chuckle.

"Ummm... It will be my term of respect for you, otherwise, you get to be Tyler." Storm retorted with a smile, and the two friends laughed at their silliness.

Ben, meanwhile, sat back and watched the two friends. So, he though, this is what it looks when brothers choose each other, rather than being thrown together by Nature. He smiled and looked over at Storm. Excellent, goodness knows nature couldn't have chosen any better.

"Is that Lucy Lou over by the door?" Tyler asked.

"Yep. She's getting to be pretty big, isn't she?" Ben replied.

"Who's Lucy Lou?" Storm asked, while looking at the small cat by the door.

"She's my daughter." Ben replied, "She's a year old and is expecting her first litter."

"Really!?" Tyler exclaimed with excitement, "I didn't know that."

"We just found out. And you have been a bit busy lately, what with the whole 'fire thing'." Ben laughed, as he turned Tyler's words from earlier back on him.

For a moment the three friends looked at each other, then burst out laughing.

"Okay, fine. I get the point, I'll come visit more often." Tyler laughed, "Now, what seems to be the issue, why did you want us out here? And, while we're at it, where are the rest of the cats?" Tyler asked after looking around.

"Well, that's kind of the point." Ben sighed, "Some of the cats are in the barn sleeping, but many have left."

"Left? Why?" Storm said, confused by not knowing the ways of the farm.

"Well, Storm," Ben said in his quiet way, "It's not unusual for cats to leave the farm. They go to other farms to find mates. Otherwise, everyone would be related, and we wouldn't grow. But that's only part of the issue." he paused and looked over at the farm in the distance.

"That's the problem." Ben continued, "The dogs."

Storm and Tyler looked across the field at the other farm. It had a smaller house and barn than the one on Ben's farm, and it didn't appear to be as well kept as the one they were standing at, but still seemed to be in good shape.

Storm looked closely at the farm and noticed three dogs, two golden retrievers and what appeared to be some form of cocker spaniel.

"What? Those dogs? Who in the world would use golden's and a cocker as guard dogs?" Tyler asked incredulously.

"Actually, it's a hybrid... a cocker poodle mix, I believe it's called a cockapoo." Ben laughed, "The golden's are Hunter and Jackson, they are as sweet as two dogs can get. They're hunting dogs, trained to go out with their human. The cockapoo is Korkie, and if dogs and cats can be friends, then he really is my friend. He's great"

"Okay, so the dogs are great, what's the problem?" Tyler asked. He was confused, this didn't make any sense to him, but Ben was obviously upset.

Just then, a small dog came flying around the corner of the far farmhouse. She was larger than the cats, but smaller than the two golden's. About the same size as Korkie, but much thinner. She had long pointed ears, a long, sharp snout and long legs, and appeared to be completely out of control. She ran around yapping and literally bouncing as she ran around the barnyard.

"What..." Storm asked as he stared at the small dog, "is that?"

"That..." Ben replied with a long sigh, "is Emily!"

"Umm... okay." Tyler started, "But, what is she?"

"Well, the best we can figure out, she is another hybrid. We are pretty sure she is a combination of rat terrier and Australian cattle dog." Ben said, "The family that bought the farm over there got her a while ago. Since then, she has been making life a terror around here. She has driven off many of the cats in the area by her aggressiveness and constant yapping. The cats simply can't abide her. Several asked if we couldn't just kill her and be done with it, but that's not the way I run the farms around here. Violence won't solve things." Ben sighed again. This was getting hard. Controlling all the cats around all the local farms, while constantly dealing with that crazy dog. And now, the cats were simply leaving. Soon, they would be having mice and rat problems around the farm again.

"Ben," Tyler started, "I don't disagree that violence isn't the answer, but as we have talked a million times, sometimes you have to protect what's yours." he said calmly to his brother.

"That's not my way Tyler. And it isn't your way, either, we don't use violence to solve things. But, you are right, sometimes we have to be more aggressive, and I guess that's why I asked you here, you're better at it than I am." Ben said softly.

"Aggression through proxy?" Storm asked incredulously.

"No, I just mean without violence. But you and Tyler spend all your time solving problems. I thought... well, maybe you could help us find a solution that doesn't include killing that nutcase over there." Ben chuckled nervously.

"Of course we'll help." Tyler said, "But we'll need time to figure this out."

At this point, Storm burst out laughing. Ben and Tyler stared at him, "What he heck is up with you?" they asked in unison.

"Well, I was just thinking. We have a dog problem. You know what we need?"

At this Tyler burst out laughing as well. Ben looked at them like they were crazy. Then, he realized what they must be thinking. He had heard that they had a friend who was a gigantic, black and white akita. "You're thinking of..."

"Yes," Tyler and Storm said at the same time, and all three cats simultaneously said one name. "Keiko!"

Three

Keiko sat quietly in a patch of warm sunshine in the backyard of the home she shared with her human. She didn't mind the collar around her neck, or the nylon leash that tied her to the building. She was a kept dog, and loved her life. Plus, she knew that she, or one of her cat friends, could chew through the leash in seconds if another emergency cropped up.

At over a hundred pounds, and standing over three feet high at the shoulder, she was one of the biggest dogs in the city. As an akita, she was a bit of an anomaly, she had a long coat, and a huge grey mane. She was, all agreed, the most beautiful dog around.

She also had another uniqueness. Her closest friends were cats. Lots of them. And she would give her life for them. Almost had during the fire. But then, she had to help Storm, after what he and CB had done to get the animals out of the fire, they deserved anything she do to help them.

As she sat quietly, chewing on a bone, she saw her two best friends come walking around the corner of the house, accompanied by a third cat she had never seen before.

Storm reached her first and, as had become their habit, rested his forehead against hers in silence for a couple seconds, "How are you, my big furry friend?" Storm laughed.

"Doing great, fuzz butt." Keiko replied.

"Yeah, well, mine is not the only butt around here with fuzz on it." Storm laughed.

"Well, now that's a unique greeting." Ben laughed.

"Yeah, that's Storm and Keiko for you. They share a unique bond." Tyler chuckled as he stepped forward.

"How are you, Keiko?" Tyler asked.

"Doing great, thanks to you. Have I thanked you recently for finding a new life for me?" Keiko smiled.

"No need for thanks, I'm just glad this worked out." Tyler replied.

"Umm... not to interrupt, but what does she mean, you gave her a new life?" Ben asked.

"Oh, sorry. Keiko, this is my brother, Ben." Tyler said, "You see, Ben, Keiko had a rather checkered past due to some really nasty humans she lived with. I was fortunate enough to know about the human in this house, and her passion for akitas. It was an easy job getting the two of them together."

"Don't let him fool you, CB changed my life and gave me a new world to live in. It's nice to meet you. Are you really CB's brother?" Keiko said.

"Yes, I am. It's nice to finally meet you, I've heard a lot about you." Ben said softly.

"Well, welcome to my home, it's great to meet you. What can I help you gentlemen with?"

"We have a bit of a problem, and could really use your help." and with that the three friends quickly outlined their problem.

When they finished, Keiko shook her head slowly, "Humans! What are you going to do? The really need to stop combining breeds that they don't know enough about."

"What do you mean, Keiko?" Ben asked.

"Well, you have Australian cattle dogs. A working dog, who is bred to herd cattle. And you have rat terriers. A working dog, who is bred to seek out and kill rats. If that dog isn't working all day, every day, she'll go insane. Humans really need to be careful." Keiko shook her head.

For a moment Storm and Tyler looked at each other with their minds reeling, then Tyler said quietly, "So, if I understand you correctly, you're saying that the best thing for Emily is to be busy."

"Right. She has to use the strengths that Nature gave her." Keiko replied.

Again the cats looked over at each other, thinking it through. Then as if a lightbulb came on to all of them at the same time, the three cats and the dog burst out laughing.

"Do you think we can?" Ben asked.

"Oh, yeah. No problem." Storm replied.

"What a great idea." Keiko laughed.

"Storm, run down to the docks, if you would, and have Rocky and Herbie come for a visit to the alley." Tyler chuckled.

With a headbutt and fond thanks to Keiko, the three cats headed out. Ben and Tyler going back to the alley, and Storm on his way to the docks,

Four

Tyler and Ben stood in the field of the farm neighboring theirs. Three of the dogs were lazing in the sun. Emily could not be seen, but could be heard in the woods on the far side of the farm. This was a good opportunity for the two cats to chat with the three dogs. Slowly, they approached the dogs.

"Excuse us." Ben said in his usual soft voice.

The three dogs looked up slowly. These were not young dogs, Tyler knew, but at least Jackson, the youngest, should have been more animated.

"How can we help you?" Hunter asked.

Tyler was a bit taken aback by the lackadaisical response, but sat quietly to let Ben take the lead.

"My name is Ben, I live on the farm across the field. This is my brother, Tyler." he began, "We were wondering if we could have a few minutes of your time, while Emily is busy." at this, Tyler saw the three dogs give a slight shudder and quickly glanced around them.

"She's not around, is she?" Korkie said with a quiver in his voice.

Ben and Tyler exchanged a glance, and understanding flashed between them. These dogs weren't old, they were beaten. Ben leaned over and whispered in Tyler's ear, "You know, Tyler, I don't think anyone has physically harmed these dogs. I think they are mentally beaten, broken might be a better word."

"I agree, and I am pretty sure Emily is is the key." Tyler whispered back.

Ben turned back to the three dogs, "No, I don't think she's done chasing, well... whatever it is she's chasing in the woods. I don't mean to be bold, but I think we have the same problem. You see, there used to be dozens of cats in the neighboring farms. But once Emily came along, she has been driving them out. No cats on a farm means more mice and rats. Now, that works fine for you here, because Emily will take care of the problem here, but it is not the case on the other farms." he said with his usual, calm patience.

"Cats aren't the only thing she's driving... she's driving us crazy. All that constant running around and yapping. We're losing our minds." Hunter said. He was an older dog, with his deep golden color being almost red, but with grey around his eyes and muzzle. This was a dog getting ready to retire, not ready to start a new fight.

"Well," CB said calmly, "maybe we can work together to find a solution."

"We thought about smothering her in her sleep, but we really aren't violent dogs." Jackson said with a laugh, which got the whole group laughing.

Finally, Korkie spoke up, "Shhhh, we need to be quiet before she hears us. What is this plan you have in mind?"

"Well, the details of the plan we can save for later, quite honestly we would rather not have to get to that point, but I kind of think we need to start by talking to her." CB said.

"Ohhhh... I see." Korkie said with a sigh, "You're one of those crazy cats. Trust me, you don't want to talk to her, she's insane."

Again the gang got to laughing, "I know, I hear you. But it only seems fair to try talking first."

"Well, you are about to get your chance, here she comes." Hunter said.

CB turned to look and, sure enough, Emily was charging out of the trees, heading directly towards them, yelling incoherently. He looked over at Ben and their new friends and said softly, "Well, here we go." just then Emily arrived.

* * *

"Who are you? Why are you here? Why are you talking to these dogs? Why are you on my property? What do cats want with us? Why would cats come onto property with dogs?..."

All of these questions and a dozen more were fired at the cats with amazing speed, as the little dog bounced up and down and ran around in circles. Tyler looked over at Ben with his jaw agape. He had never seen anything like Emily before. Ben, for his part, was looking at the three dogs laying quietly a slight distance from the whirling dervish that was Emily. The dogs seemed to be crawling backward to get away from the barrage of sound. And still the questions kept coming from Emily.

"Hey, you look familiar, aren't you from the farm next door? Didn't all the cats from that farm leave? Where did they all go? How come there aren't as many as there used to be? Won't that mean more mice and rats at your farm?..." she continued.

As Tyler and Ben opened their mouths to try and stop the deluge of questions by the bouncing dog, another voice joined the fray.

"Holy smokes, doesn't she ever shut up?" Ben and Tyler spun around to see Storm standing next to them with a look of awe on his face. Emily didn't seem to notice the new cat in the mix, she just kept firing questions and comments while bouncing up and down.

It was Hunter who answered, "Nope. This is what we deal with all day. She just goes on and on. Is there anything you can do to help?"

At this point, Ben tried a more direct approach, "Emily, we came to talk to you about the farms." but it was clear that Emily never even heard him. She just kept talking and bouncing.

Tyler tried a bit more forcefully, "Emily, can you please stop talking long enough for us to discuss the farms with you?" he said with his voice raised. Again it appeared he might as well be talking to himself for all the response he got from Emily. He noticed, however, that she was getting a bit more aggressive and bouncing toward them. He could see how she had driven off the other cats in the area, if she got too assertive, she could easily hurt a cat.

Storm, in his usual way, was much less subtle. "SHUT UP!!!" he yelled at the crazy bounding dog. This, for the first time got her to pause in her diatribe, but even that was only for a second, then she started up again.

She was getting closer to the cats, and her non-stop chatter was being punctuated with low growls. The three cats looked at each other, then over at the three dogs, "You guys had better leave, she will get violent in a few minutes."

"Right." Ben said, "We'll be back when we have a plan to help you out,"

At this, the three cats turned and ran back to their own property. Behind them, Emily started to chase them, then was distracted by a squirrel and ran off in a different direction.

* * *

Back at their farm, it was Storm who spoke first. "CB, she's crazy! There's no way we can deal with her." he said, clearly agitated. It was obvious that the frenetic energy of the dog had affected the cats. They were all on edge.

"You know what, Storm?" Ben said, "I actually agree with you. As much as I like to think that there is always a peaceful resolution to problems, I don't think there is for this case."

"Unfortunately, I agree as well." Tyler said. "I hate to say it, I was really hoping we could avoid implementing our plan, but I guess we don't have a choice." he said with a sigh.

Storm, who had finally settled down, gave a slow sigh, "Yeah, we're all ready to go. Herbie and Rocky have all the pieces in place, they are just waiting for the word. You do know that concessions will have to be made, right?"

"Yeah," Tyler said with a sigh, "I know, but it seems to be worth it. We can't let this continue. The cats need to come back to the farms, and those three dogs need a break."

"When do you want to move forward?" Ben asked.

"We can be ready tomorrow." Storm said.

The three cats looked at each other and shook their heads, "All right, let's go." Tyler said. As they walked away Tyler looked over at Emily's farm. She continued to run around, barking and harassing the other dogs. He had hoped he could do his differently, but there was no choice. Life on the farms was about to change drastically.

Five

The sun was just cresting the horizon as the three cats returned to the farm. It had been a long night, spent putting the final touches on the plan for putting some reigns on Emily. The friends were tired and frustrated. None of them truly wanted to put the plan in play. There were too may concessions and potentials for things to go very bad for them.

Ultimately, it was Ben who made the final decision. His years of running the farms in the area had taught him well, and he knew that in the long run the cats would return to the farms and some level of control could be regained.

Some thought had been given to having Keiko make an attempt to get through to Emily, but even she knew that it would be wasted effort. Emily wasn't a behavioral problem, she was a genetic problem. The way she acted had nothing to do with how she was raised, it was all about how she was bred. She needed to work, and herd and hunt.

With a quick glance at each other, the three cats began the slow stroll over to where Emily had already been let out and was running around barking. When they reached the edge of the farm, they were met by a large, brown rat.

On any other day, this would have led to a fight, and a snack for the cats, but this time, the cats greeted the rat cordially.

"Good morning, Allo." Tyler said quietly, "Thanks for coming. As you know, we greatly regret that it had to come to this. I assume the terms are acceptable to you."

Allo grinned lightly and said, "Glad I could help out, Mr. CB. Herbie and Rocky explained the plan, we are so glad we can help out."

CB smiled. Allo was a good animal, as rats went, but he was definitely not the brightest creature he had ever met, "Fine. But do not forget that the farm we offer is the only farm we offer. If you stray beyond its boundaries, other than to come back to this farm and address the issue of Emily as needed, you will face every cat we can raise. And remember, Allo, the other three dogs are to be left alone." CB said with a laugh.

"Ah, yeah, sure we get that." Allo said with a laugh, "We rats ain't got no beef with you cats, we just gonna be glad to have use of that farm. The docks are getting a bit crowded."

"Yes, I know. We are constantly having to work on keeping the docks organized, we'll be glad to split you guys up a bit." CB said with a chuckle.

As they chatted, the three cats and the one rat finished the short walk to Emily's farm, and Allo moved out into the field. As Emily saw the cats, she rushed over and started to attack. Storm stepped in front of her with his hackles up, hissing and spitting, Tyler and Ben did the same, and in seconds the fight was on. Emily ran around and bounced, while nipping at the cats, Storm took a frontal approach and managed to get his claws on Emily's ear, while Tyler came around her flank and sank his teeth on her hind leg. She wiggled free and was renewing her attack when Ben entered the fray. At full speed he hit Emily broadside and tumbled her over. While she was down, and catching her breath, Ben took the opportunity to try talking to her.

"Emily, please stop this, we need to work together." he said in his quiet way.

"Work together, never. You need to get off my property." she said quickly.

"Fine, but then you need to stay off our property." Ben replied.

"All property is my property. It's my job to chase you away." Emily said quickly.

"That can't work, Emily. We have to take care of our own property, and you have to take care of yours. And leave us alone." Ben said.

"Nope." Emily replied. "Everything I see, I control. That includes you. It's my job." with that reply she jumped at Storm without warning, but Storm had been expecting it. Taking a play from Tyler's book, he countered the move and all Emily found when she got to where he had been was an empty space, and felt a smack on the back of her head that made her see stars.

Before she could renew her attack again, Tyler jumped in, "Stop this, all of you. Cats, move back. Emily stop." he said with a growl, and everyone stopped. He turned to Emily and didn't hesitate to let his anger show, "We have tried to do this the easy way. We have tried to be pleasant and work with you. You obviously refuse. So now it's time for us to take over." he said.

"Just try taking over, cat." Emily replied with a growl. As she started to move toward Tyler again, she saw him motion with his paw, and saw a rat in the field.

As her instincts started to take over she saw something she could not believe.

* * *

Allo watched the fight with amazement. He had known CB for years, and knew Storm as well. But he had never met Ben before. He knew Ben was a bit of a pacifist, but who would have thought he could fight the way he did. For a moment he took CB's words to heart, maybe it was not a good idea to start a fight with the cats.

As the fight settled down and a semblance of conversation took place, he expected a peaceful outcome. But when Emily would not back down, he saw CB give a signal with his paw. Slowly he stood up on his hind legs so Emily could see him. As she moved forward to attack as her breeding had taught her, he gave a small signal of his own. What Emily saw next brought her to a halt.

* * *

Storm watched as Tyler gave his signal to Allo. He saw Allo stand up on his hind legs, saw Emily ready for the attack and then saw something he never expected. Initially, his reaction was to prepare to fight, then he burst out laughing.

Sure, he thought to himself, Allo may not be very smart, but surely even he couldn't make a mistake this gigantic.

With a quick glance he saw that Tyler and Ben were as shocked as he was, and this led him to laugh even harder. If Emily had attacked him then, he would be dead in a second.

It was all in Tyler's hands now. As he laughed, he sat back on his haunches and waited to see what Tyler did.

***

Tyler took in the scene in a second. Ben was shocked, Storm had burst out laughing and was essentially worthless, Emily was stunned into immobility with Nature telling her to attack and reality telling her to stop.

With a sigh, he turned his attention to Allo, "Ummm... Allo... I know I asked you to bring some of your rats with you, so we could give Emily work to do, other than attacking the cats and other dogs on the farms. Our hope was that she would be so busy chasing you folks, that she wouldn't have time to bother anyone else... but, exactly what did you tell your rats?"

"I told them we needed a hundred rats to come with us. Why?" Allo said with a confused look on his face.

"I see." Tyler replied, trying not to start laughing himself, "Did you happen to mention to them that you needed a TOTAL of a hundred rats?" he asked.

"Uhhh, I'm not sure, why do you ask?" Allo replied.

"Well... look!" Tyler said and pointed behind Allo. Allo spun around and was stunned at what he saw.

At Allo's signal rats had begun crawling out of the fields and the forest by the tens, then hundreds, then thousands and then the hundreds of thousands. Tyler and the team had never seen so many rats. What started as a trickle soon resembled a moving brown blanket covering the fields.

Allo let out a shriek and yelled at the rats to stop. "Wait! Stop! Holy Smokes, what did you do?" he yelled at his main assistants.

"What? You told us to find a hundred rats and come out to the farms." one of them exclaimed.

"Yikes!!! I didn't mean for ALL of you to find a hundred rats, just a grand total of a hundred." he turned and looked at Tyler, Ben, Storm and all the dogs. Emily was paralyzed, Ben and Tyler had a look of disbelief and a hint of humor, and Storm was laughing so hard he was rolling across the grass with tears running down his face.

"I, ummm... I think you can send some of them home, we really won't need that many." Ben said in his calmest, quietest voice. At which, Storm lost all control in his fit of laughter and Tyler couldn't hold it in any longer. He also burst out laughing.

Six

When the laughter stopped and the majority of the rats had gone home, Tyler turned his attention to Emily.

"So," he said calmly, "you want to work, huh? Fine, here's what we'll do. We cats have given the rats the full run of the old farm about a mile down the road. You know the one, with the huge abandoned silo full of corn, and the soy growing wild in the fields. The cats will make sure that the population of rats stays fairly consistent and doesn't overrun the farm. And the rats, as payment for the farm, will come here daily and keep you so busy chasing them that you won't have the opportunity to bother anyone else. From today forward, the only job, and the only control, you will have, is keeping your yard free of the rats. Their job, will be to assure that they send enough of their populace here every day that you won't ever bother the cats, or the other dogs, again. Is that clear?"

Emily stared at him in shock. For so long, she had felt she was in such great control, that it was hard for her to absorb that that had all changed. She looked from Tyler, to Ben, to Storm and back again. In an instant, she realized she had lost the battle, "But... ummm... how long do you plan for this to continue?" Emily asked in a stunned voice.

"We will keep an eye on things, and if you improve your behavior and attitude, we'll renegotiate at that time." Ben said softly, "To begin with, leave these dogs alone, or I swear to you that the rats will be the least of your problems."

"Really? What could be worse?" Emily exclaimed.

"Well, to begin with, we can send back ALL the rats. But beyond that, didn't we tell you? Keiko is one of our closest friends." Ben said.

Emily let out a shriek. Keiko's reputation as the biggest and toughest dog in the area had preceded her, how was Emily to know that, underneath, Keiko was the sweetest animal in the region, "You wouldn't send her here, would you?" Emily cried.

"Follow the rules and, no we won't. Don't follow the rules and...." Tyler replied, letting the end of the sentence lapse.

"Fine." Emily said with a sigh, "Meanwhile, if there are no other rules, I really need to get to work getting all these rats off my property." and with that she ran off towards the corn field barking loudly.

Ben, Tyler and Storm turned to the three dogs, who were all sitting quietly, smiling, "Thank you," Hunter said, "That was brilliant. We owe you one."

"Our pleasure." Tyler said, "Whatever we can do to help."

"You know," Storm added, with a smile "if you guys are up for some exercise, I think Emily could use a hand."

Hunter looked over at Jackson and Korkie who were laying comfortably in the shade of the house, listening to Emily running around in the field chasing rats, "You know, that's a great idea. We'll do that. Well, after a long nap, of course." he said, and again the whole team fell into a fit of laughter.

Seven

Keiko wiped tears of laughter from her eyes as she listened to Tyler and Storm explain what had occurred at the farm.

"Oh, my goodness, what was Allo thinking?" she howled.

"I kind of think that's the point." Storm replied, "He wasn't thinking."

Tyler tried to catch his breath from laughing, but the mental picture in his head stopped him and he choked, "I swear to you," he cried, "I have never see that many rats in one place in my whole life. Heck, I didn't even know there were that many rats."

"I know," Storm said through his laughs, "I will never forget the look on poor Emily's face. If she were a cat, I think she would have lost four of her lives when she saw all those rats come through the fields."

"Well, I sure wish I could have been there to see that." Keiko said with a chuckle.

"Yeah, it was quite a scene." Tyler said. "I knew it was a great idea as soon as you gave us a hint about what her nature told her to do. Even so, I really didn't plan to overwhelm her quite to that level."

"Well, it isn't like you intended that, but still, I do think your point was made." Keiko said with a chuckle.

"Yeah, I guess. Still, overall, I think we did well. But as I think about it, I wonder if we shouldn't keep an eye on her." Storm said, suddenly serious.

"I agree. Especially since we are clear about the intellectual level of the rats. It won't take much for them to forget their boundaries." Tyler replied.

"I talked to Ben just before we left, and he said he has word out to all the cats in the area that they could return to the farms. He said that about a dozen had already told him they were coming back. They are talking to a few dozen others. He expects they will be able to keep the rat population under control... and get a little extra protein in their diet as well." Storm said with a smile.

"Still," Keiko said, "I agree that we should keep an eye on this. Emily could get fairly overwhelmed by this and will need some support. As nice as those other dogs sound, they are not rat terriers, they won't be as good at fighting off the rats. So, they are likely to just give up and leave it to her. Maybe, ultimately, we will need to make a change in our plans." the big dog said.

"We'll watch her carefully," Tyler said, "and make sure she doesn't get hurt. However, it would be good if there were some way you could go visit her once in a while, Keiko."

"Well, now that you mention it, there has been a bit of a change on that level. My human knows how much I love sitting in the yard, so several times a week she leaves me outside for a few hours, and doesn't keep as close an eye on me as she used to. Also, I figured out how to get my chain off without chewing through it. So, I can get free regularly and head out to the farm. It's not really a long run from here and I need the exercise."

"It's a deal then, we'll keep an eye on her and you can go out give her support regularly." Tyler said.

"Good, that's settled then." Storm said, "Now, what else is new?" he asked.

As the sun settled on what had been a very long day, Keiko, Storm and Tyler settled down for a quiet chat amongst old friends. Anyone listening in Keiko's neighborhood would have been entertained by the sound of a large dog and two cats chatting and laughing quietly.

The Cat Burglar:
Exodus

One

Storm sat huddled in the corner of the entryway which he and CB shared in the alley, staring out at the rain. It had been pouring down rain for three days, and Storm felt soaked to the skin, even though he had not been out in the rain itself for hours.

This was not one of those gentle drizzles that can be a bit annoying, there had been an all out deluge going on non-stop day in and day out, and everyone had had about enough of it. A little water was a good thing. What they had seen over the past few days was ridiculous.

With a sigh, he glanced over at CB sitting in his big, overstuffed chair and saw the same tired frustration on his friends face, "So..." Storm started, only to be cut off by CB.

"Storm, stop. I can't take another diatribe about how much you are sick of the rain. If you find some way for me to solve the problem, by all means, let me know, and I will be happy to oblige. If not, then take a deep breath, accept that it will stop raining when it stops raining, and move on!" he said in a huff.

"Wow! And you think I'm in a bad mood. Yikes." Storm chuckled, "Okay, I admit, I have been a bit whiney lately. Sorry." Storm said with a sigh, "But, what I was going to say was... 'So, I see Jaffa is having fun entertaining the gang this morning.'"

Over the past year, Jaffa had taken on the role of the storyteller for the cats. Who knew that the scared little cat from The Heights who had sought out CB for help, would become such an integral part of the team. Every day he would leave his warm and comfortable home, and come to the alley to spend time with his friends, laughing, joking and telling stories.

Today, Jaffa was telling the story he had heard about the day CB caught a rogue cat stealing fish from a restaurant down on the waterfront. The little cat had eaten so much that when he tried to run away, he couldn't get through the hole he had used to get in. CB recruited him and paired him with Rocky to patrol the docks.

Storm laughed at the story, and the way Jaffa told it. All of that had happened long before Storm joined the team, but he had known the team at the dock for quite a while now and found them to be some of the nicest and hardest working cats he had ever met.

"Sorry." CB said with a laugh, "I guess I am also a little touchy after all this rain. My concern is the flooding that is starting here in Jones. There are some houses in pretty desperate shape down there." word was traveling fast about whole neighborhoods of Jones being washed away.

"We need to keep an eye on the situation. When the humans get evacuated from the area, it opens up opportunities for other humans to break in and steal things." CB said.

"Yeah, I understand that." Storm said, "But I'm not sure what we can do to help that situation. We are too small, we would just get washed away by the flood."

"I agree, and I have no answer either, but we need to keep an eye on it." CB said with a sigh.

"My bigger concern is closer to home." Storm said, "This alley is fairly well protected from the rain, but these buildings are old, and the flow of water is increasing along the east side."

"I have been thinking the same thing. We need to start thinking about moving out of here for a while, if this continues. We should at least have a plan in place."

"Agreed. But where. I talked to Keiko yesterday, and she said her yard looks like a lake, and she is remaining indoors most of the time now. Ben's farm is safe, but with all their cats back, there's no room. Emily's farm has already flooded, and she and her family have moved out to a friends farm a few miles out of town. Jaffa's neighborhood is still fairly dry, since it's up on a hill, with good drainage, but we can't take a couple dozen cats to his courtyard." Storm sighed.

"Hmmm... I talked to Paradise and she has the same summary. Her neighborhood is high enough to be safe, but there is nowhere that we can just drop off dozens of cats without drawing attention." CB said.

"The docks might be an option, but if the humans suddenly see dozens of cats marching on the docks, they're going to start exterminating us. We need some place that is high, relatively dry and is hidden enough that we won't draw attention." Storm looked over at Jaffa and the rest of the team. These are good animals, kind, caring and loyal. But they are still animals, when pushed too far, they will find a way to lash out if it is needed to survive. Jaffa can keep them distracted with stories, and CB can control them with his leadership, but eventually their instinct to fight or fly will take over. The cats could easily get killed if they rushed out without thinking.

"Yeah, but where? Ben was here yesterday and told me about a small forest he knows of, but it is another 10 miles past his farm, and other than being secluded, it is not dry and has no access to food." anxiety began to grow in CB. His team was in danger, and he couldn't figure out how to help. Part of him just hoped the rain would stop and he wouldn't have to worry any more, but his instincts told him that was not the way this would go. This rain had the feel of something that would continue for a long time. He needed a plan for his team.

Two

It was on day five of solid pouring rain, that the alley finally flooded. The building where CB and Storm made their home began to crumble at the corners, and the reality that the building could actually collapse became a certainty.

CB knew it was time to go. The question remained... where? No matter what they did, they couldn't find a safe place for anything other than a very short term fix.

It was the memory of an old conversation with Paradise that provided a solution to the problem, at least temporarily. During that chat, through a screened window, Paradise happened to mention the day that CB had searched the entire Civic Center looking for her, only to find she wasn't there.

As he thought about the craziness of that day, the idea hit CB like a thunderbolt. The new Civic Center was nearing completion, and the old Civic Center was scheduled to be destroyed. But, for the time being, neither was being used. CB could take his team into the old center and avoid the workers in the new center. There were plenty of mice for food, and they would be safe from the rain and floods.

The buildings sat on the the edge of one of the highest hills in town. As long as they stayed out of the basement, there should be no chance of finding flood waters. And, the building was still structurally sound, it was only being replaced because it was old and and out of date.

Rushing back down from the entrance of the alley, to the building he shared with Storm, CB ran into Storm who was coming to find him, "You need to hurry, CB, one of the smaller buildings in the alley just collapsed. It is leaning on our building, and so far it is holding, but it won't last long. We need to get the cats out of there, we have too many kittens and expectant mothers in the alley to risk them further." Storm said in a rush.

"Was anyone hurt with the collapse?"

"Not seriously, Jaffa and Marti were grazed by a brick when it fell, and Rocky barely missed getting hit by a door, but everyone else seems fine. We just need to move and do so soon." Storm replied.

"I have an idea where we can go. The old Civic Center is empty, and should be safe for a while. We can gather everyone together and head there."

"Great idea. The only problem is, it's a couple miles away, the storm is getting stronger and all of the roads heading to it are washed out by the floods." Storm sighed.

"We can do it, it's the only safe place I can think of. What we really need is size and strength. Can you get to Keiko and see if she can help out?" CB asked.

"Sure, I'll try, but I think her house is on the edge of the flood. She may be trapped inside." Storm replied.

"Gotta try, go and see, and meet us back here." CB said as he started to run down the alley, "Oh, and Storm!"

"What?" Storm stopped and turned back to CB.

"Be careful."

"Good advice, you too."

Three

When Storm arrived at Keiko's house, he found the yard empty. With all the rain, and Keiko's extra long and thick fur, her human had kept her in the house most of the day. The trick was to get her out, and away from the house, without her human wondering where she was.

A quick surveillance of the house showed that Keiko was in the living room and her human was in the hallway putting on her jacket, "Well, that's a start anyway." Storm thought, at least her human was leaving. Now, the question was how to get her out of the house.

As soon as he saw the car pull away from the house, Storm ran up to the window in the living room and scratched at the screen. Keiko responded immediately.

"Storm! What it the world are you doing out in this weather?" Keiko exclaimed.

"We need help, the alley is flooding, and the buildings are coming down. We need to get the cats to a safe place, but the kittens and some of the mothers are too small and weak to move. Is there any way you can get out of there, we need size and strength to get over the flooded parts of the city, to shelter."

"Where do you expect to find shelter from this?" Keiko asked.

"CB thinks the old Civic Center will work temporarily, but we will eventually need a permanent new home." Storm said.

"Well, my human will be gone for about 10 hours, let me think how I can get out of here." Keiko said as she began wandering the house. She didn't want to break a window, she needed a way to get out and back in without her human knowing, though how she would dry all that fur later was something she would consider when the time came.

Eventually, she came upon the back door, the one she usually went out when she was put on the leash for the day. She had dealt with doors before, but bursting through them was not very inconspicuous. She looked at the lock and realized it was a fairly simple mechanism. All she had to do was turn the small lock, then turn the handle and pull.

Since her head was already at door handle level, it did not take any effort to reach the small lock. Gripping it in her front teeth, she turned it so it was pointed sideways, rather than up and down. Then, adjusting her grip, she took the entire handle in her mouth. With a turn of her head, the handle turned and the bolt unlatched from the frame. A quick pull and she was faced by a second door.

This door was much easier. All she had to do was reach up with a paw and hit the small latch type handle and the door bounced open. She was free. As she started to step out the door, she realized that if she let the door go, it would latch behind her and she would not be able to get it open again from the outside.

At the same time, Storm came running around the house carrying a small stick which he dropped at Keiko's feet, "I figured that if you got the door open, you might want something to prop it open, so it didn't close and you could get back in." the small cat said.

"We'll, that's you and I thinking alike again. Lean that stick against the door frame, just where the door would meet it." Keiko instructed.

Storm took the small stick, and holding it against the frame of the open door allowed Keiko to slowly close the door. The weight of the door pressed against the stick, which in turn pressed against the frame, and the door was effectively propped in an open position. All Keiko had to do was pull on the door, the stick would fall and she could slip back in the open door.

"Excellent, Storm. Now, let's go see what we can do to help the cats." Keiko said as the two friends rushed off toward the alley.

Four

CB found himself confronted with chaos. Jaffa, Herbie and Rocky had managed to get the cats organized in safe areas of the alley, but the alley itself looked like a bomb had gone off in it. Three buildings had collapsed, and two others were leaning, while a river of water ran through the entire area. CB was amazed at the destruction caused by the flood, but even more so by the fact that none of the cats had been harmed... or killed,

"Where are we, guys?" CB asked of his leaders.

"Everyone is safe." Rocky replied, "But we won't be for long. The whole alley is very close to washing out completely. These buildings were never very stable to begin with, but now they are downright dangerous. We need to get out of here."

"We're working on that. Storm is over at Keiko's to see if she can help. In the meantime, get everyone ready to move as soon as it gets a little darker. We can't move as a group during daylight, without alerting the humans of our organizational skills, and I will not allow anyone to travel on their own. We stay together, we travel together, and hopefully, we all stay alive together." CB replied.

"Yeah, but where?" Jaffa asked.

"To the old Civic Center. It's above the water line, and is vacant. No one will know we're there."

"Great plan. But half the roads are washed out getting there." Jaffa said.

"I know. My thought is to head up toward The Heights, then go around the downtown area and back up the hill to the Civic Center. And, Jaffa, when we get to The

Heights, you get back into your human's house and stay safe." CB said.

"CB, no, I need to help." Jaffa cried.

"No, Jaffa, you need to be safe. No heroes today, just safety."

"Okay, fine. I understand." Jaffa said, "But, I have an idea. You said that Keiko may be here. What if we take all the kittens and mothers and put them in that metal trash container over there. We can wrap a rope around the handles and Keiko can pull the rope with her teeth."

CB stared at Jaffa in amazement, "You know, Jaffa, you keep proving yourself to be that brilliant and I may not allow you to go home."

"Oh, CB, I'm just trying to help." Jaffa stammered.

"Keep it up. OKAY, LISTEN UP EVERYONE." CB yelled, "I WANT EVERYONE WHO CAN, TO GET OVER TO THE KITTENS AND MOMS. I WANT THEM IN THAT BIG METAL TRASH BIN... THE ONE WITH THE WHEELS. ALSO, GET SOME DRY BLANKETS IN THERE IF WE HAVE ANY."

Herbie came running up and said, "CB, I heard what you're planning, and I think I can help with the rope. I brought some up from the docks a while back, just in case we needed it. With a bit of help I can get it tied to the handles. Can I steal Jaffa from you?"

"Go. And get the rest of the cats ready to move as soon as..." CB stopped as he saw Storm come running around the corner, with a giant dog following behind. "... well, as soon as those two get here." he chuckled.

CB quickly updated Storm and Keiko on the plan, and in minutes they were ready to go.

When all the preparations were in place, CB gathered all the cats, "Alright, everyone, we're in for a long night. Only bring what we absolutely need. We'll have to find new materials in the future. Herbie, I want you and ten of the cats to head out first, get to the center and get the entryway open for us. Also, scour around and find anything you can that will act as bedding for the kittens and mothers."

"No problem, boss." he said.

"Good, go. Rocky, take six others with you and get to the docks. Make sure the cats there are safe, and if not, get them to the Civic Center. Everyone else stays with me, Storm and Keiko. Under no circumstances does anyone travel alone. Teams, stay together."

"YES, SIR." came the reply.

"Alright, team, let's go." CB said.

Five

As the flood continued to wash out their home, the cats of the alley began a slow march around the river that had replaced what was once their whole world.

Keiko ran over to the metal trash can and lifted the plastic lid. Inside we're eight mother cats and over twenty of the cutest kittens she had ever seen. The cats and kittens were well familiar with the big dog, from all her visits. No one was scared of her.

"Okay, little ones, we are heading out for a bit of a journey. I won't lie, it's going to be bumpy. Just relax and enjoy the ride."

Closing the lid, she walked to the end of the looped rope. Each end of the rope was tied to a handle on either side of the trash bin, and allowed Keiko to step inside the loop, and grab the center of it with her teeth, while the two sides of the rope ran along her sides. She looked like a horse, harnessed to a wagon.

Once she had the rope set comfortably in her teeth, she took her first step. The trash bin was heavy, but not terribly so, and the wheels moved easily. The ropes being attached to each handle gave it plenty of stability and she was quickly able to get the bin moving.

"Okay, gang. Let's go." CB said.

They had already moved to the entrance of the alley, to get away from the flood and collapsing buildings, so leaving the alley was an easy process. As they took the first steps, Storm and CB both stopped and looked behind them. The alley was their home, and now their lives there were over.

"I'm sorry, CB. I know how hard you worked to create this world for us." Storm said softly.

"We'll do it again, Storm. We just need to find a new place. It is very sad though." CB said. As if to put the final closure on the situation, as Storm and CB turned back to the others, they heard the doorway they had shared collapse.

"We need to go, before this whole alley crumbles and kills us all." Storm said.

Night had fallen and with the storm raging, the street lights had all been knocked out, so they could travel unobserved.

Their first problem was crossing the street that ran perpendicular to the alley, so they could continue straight up the hill. Water ran down the center of the street half a foot deep. For cats, most of whom were only about eight inches tall to the top of their backs, this was a daunting challenge.

Keiko had the solution to this problem. By pulling the trash bin into the street, the wheels caused the water to disperse and lowered the level. The cats were then able to run across. When they were across, Keiko pulled the bin the rest of the way.

"CB, we're going to have to stay on the edge of the road as we go up." Keiko said, "There's no way I can pull this thing over the grass."

"That's fine for now, we just need to go uphill for a couple blocks, are you going to be okay with that?" Storm asked.

"Yeah, strength isn't a problem, fortunately this thing has a lot of plastic on it, so it's not completely steel.

My concern is this rope. It's thin, I'm concerned about biting through it."

"Wow, I hadn't thought about that. I'll see if we can find some stronger rope." Storm replied.

A block later, Keiko's concern was getting deeper. The weight of the bin, and the steepness of the hill were causing her to bite harder to maintain control, and again she expressed her concern, "The rope is starting to fray where my teeth have hold of it." she said quietly.

Jaffa looked around at the rubble which had been carried along with the flood. There were bits of metal, paper and stones everywhere he looked, but not what he was seeking. Frantically, he kept searching.

Finally, on the side of the road, he found what he was looking for. A piece of old towel, or blanket, had been washed down the road with the flood and a bunch of other junk. Asking Keiko to drop the rope for a moment, he asked CB to help him, and together they wrapped the towel around the rope, making a large bundle for Keiko to grab. When Keiko picked it back up, she found it was much thicker, and she was able to hold it more firmly.

CB smiled at the little cat and gave him a quick headbutt, "You truly are amazing, little one." he said softly.

Again the gang started moving. The next major cross street they reached was high enough that they were able to cross without too much trouble, as there was only a small trickle of water running down the street, and by the time they reached the top of the hill, they could clearly see that they were above the water line.

With a deep sigh, the team stopped and looked back at the four blocks they had just travelled, what would usually have taken less than two minutes, had taken them over half an hour.

For a full five minutes they sat and rested. There were twenty cats in their group, and CB could see that they were stressed. Turning to Storm he started going through the plan, "From here, we can stay on the level for about six blocks, then we have the big hill to go down on the other side of Jones. After that we have ten blocks to get through downtown, then up the hill to the Civic Center."

"Yep, that's the way I see it too. We should check on that rope and make sure it's sturdy before we move out again. My biggest concern is the flat stretch through Jones and into downtown. We know the floods are bad there. It sure would be nice if we could come in from above the Civic Center." Storm said.

"I agree. There are a few roads up there, but as you know, the two main ones are under construction, and really nothing much more than holes in the ground."

"Yeah, I know. Wait, what if we tried going one street above or below those two." Storm said.

"The one below washed out two days ago, and the next one up will take us half a mile out of our way." CB replied.

"Well, we can't just sit here. My vote would be to go up the extra half mile and avoid the risk of the downhill through Jones, and the added return uphill." Storm said.

"Alright, let's do it." CB said. Walking over to Keiko, he found the giant dog with her head inside the garbage bin, telling jokes to the kittens and mothers. CB heard peals of laughter rising from inside the bin, "Now, that, is a good dog!!" he said to himself.

"Alright, big girl, it's time to move. Our thought is to head further up, and catch one of the roads above the Civic Center, then come down to it, rather than going down and back up. Are you okay with that?" he asked

"Sure, I like that idea better. Though it does mean going further out of our way." Keiko said.

"Yeah, I know, but it does seem safer."

"Alright, let's go then." Keiko stuck her head back into the trash bin, "Listen up, little ones, we need to roll again. We are going to have to go over some construction, so it is going to be a bumpy ride. I'll try to find a smooth route, but it is unlikely that we'll find one. Try to wedge yourselves against the wall, and wrap up in those blankets. Maybe that will help you avoid some bruises."

Closing the lid and turning back to the rope, Keiko took a deep breath, leaned down, picked it up and started to move up the hill again. The rain poured down, soaking her heavy fur.

Six

As Herbie and his team reached the Civic Center, they stopped and took a deep breath. The trip had been daunting beyond anything they had ever imagined.

Their route had taken them through the heart of Jones, and they were stunned by the devastation there. Whole blocks of that section of town no longer existed as real housing. The residents had obviously evacuated, and the whole area looked abandoned. The few roads they could still find had turned to rivers, and the team had been required to go all they way into the downtown area before being able to head back up to the Civic Center.

Herbie turned to his closest assistant, a small brown and black female known to all as Meow Meow. While she was new to the group of cats from the alley, she had quickly become one of the strongest new team members. She was smart and street wise, two qualities which were indispensable to the team.

"Well, Meow Meow, that was quite the challenge, wasn't it?" Herbie said with a chuckle.

"Why, yes it was." she replied, "If this is the type of fun you folks get to have regularly, I think I am really going to enjoy being part of this team." she laughed.

"Yeah, well, we do try to make sure life is interesting." Herbie chuckled.

"So what do we do next?" Meow Meow asked.

"Well, first and foremost, we make sure we didn't lose anyone. There should be eleven of us, and at a quick glance, I can only see eight." Herbie replied.

"The other three are around the corner, looking for some shelter." the little female replied.

"Good idea, but we really don't need it. We will just get inside the building and not have to worry about it."

Taking Meow Meow and the rest of his group in tow, he headed around the building toward the access panel that CB and Storm had used previously when they went in search of Paradise.

They found the panel on the north side of the building, and quickly headed for it, looking forward to being out of the rain. But, when they arrived, they found that the hatch had been bolted back in place.

Herbie stared at the hatch with growing frustration, as the rain pelted him. Controlling his anger, he turned to the cats around him, "Listen up." he yelled above the sound of the pouring rain, "Split into groups of three and head out in each direction. Meow Meow and I will take the south side. We need to find a way in. Anything will work, but if you can find something close to ground level, that would be helpful. Remember we have kittens and nursing mothers that need to get inside as well. If you find something, let out your loudest yowl, we should be able to hear it over the thunder and rain."

As the group spread out, Herbie and Meow Meow ran toward the east side, which seemed to be more sheltered from the storm. From there, they ran as fast as they could to the south side. The old building was huge, running a bit over a block and a half on each side. They passed three of their team members as they ran, who were frantically searching that side of the building.

Arriving on the south end of the building, they began a close scrutiny of the brick facade. This side of the building was obviously the main entrance through which the humans would have entered the building for events. Almost all of this side of the building was taken up by huge glass doors and windows.

"Look for broken windows, or bent doors. We don't need a lot of room, of course, we cats can get through fairly small holes, but we have to make sure it isn't a jagged hole, we don't want anyone getting cut." Herbie instructed.

"Got it." Meow Meow said, and started running to the far end of the building.

Herbie began a detailed, thorough examination of the building. For a building which was marked for destruction, it seemed to be in amazingly good condition. The doors and windows were still solid, and he could not even find a single brick out of place.

About half way down the building he found an air vent and looked closely to see if it was loose, only to find it was solidly screwed shut. Continuing his search he found another vent, this one was missing two of the four screws, but the other two were solid and he could not remove them.

As he moved away from the vent, he saw Meow Meow run up, "Nothing." she said curtly, "And just for the record, I am getting sick and tired of being wet and cold!!" she said with growl in her voice.

Herbie looked at her for a second, then burst out laughing, "I could not agree more!!" he said as the two fell to the ground laughing. Slowly, some of their tension slipped away.

"Alright, back to work. We need to look more closely and see if we missed anything." he said with a smile.

Just then, he heard a loud yowl coming from the west side of the building. Glancing quickly at Meow Meow, they set out running.

When they arrived, they found that only the three cats from the east side had yet to arrive. He found the other cats gathered around an air vent which was hanging loose. As he pushed the metal plate aside, he saw the last three cats round the corner heading their direction, "Good, we're all still here." he said to himself.

With a quick look around at his team, he headed through the face plate and into the air tunnel. Inside, it was cool, but dry. A good start, he thought. Moving slowly, making sure to brush aside debris from the path as he walked, he quickly came to a T intersection. There was no light here, and he was not sure which way to go.

From the left he felt a cool breeze, and from the right he could smell something musty. A breeze meant air passage, mustiness meant stagnation. Turning to Meow Meow, he voiced his thoughts, "The building has not been used for quite a while, the air in that big, open hall should be stagnant. I'm thinking we head right." he said softly.

"True, and that breeze has a hint of the aroma of rain in it. My guess is that the air is being pulled in from an outside source. We need to head into the building, not back out." she said.

"Right it is, then." he replied.

As they turned the corner, what little light there was from the cloud obscured moon outside disappeared completely. They were in pitch black.

The tunnel they were in lead straight for twenty feet, then turned sharply left. From there, they continued for thirty feet before reaching an end at another air vent. Beyond the vent, Herbie could see a hint of light, and knew they had reached their goal. They had found the main hall of the Civic Center. Taking a deep breath, and hoping upon hope, he mumbled to the team, "Well, here goes nothing, lets hope this opens."

Turning his head, he leaned back, then rushed forward and hit the vent as hard as he could with his shoulder. There was a loud crashing sound, but no movement. Leaning back, he rushed and hit it again. Again, nothing but noise. As he lined up to hit it again, he felt a paw on his shoulder. He turned to see a gigantic cat he had only met once before. For the life of him he could not remember the cats name.

"Okay, that was fun to watch," the big cat said with a chuckle, "but how about you leave manual labor to those who are better suited for it." and with that, the big cat rushed past Herbie and hit the vent at a run with his full weight and strength behind him. The vent exploded from the opening and landed ten feet away.

"That, my little leader, is how you open a vent!" the big cat laughed.

As the group of cats poured themselves into the main hall, the reality of their safety settled in on them. For the next ten minutes laughter was the only thing that could be heard in the hall.

Seven

Rocky arrived at the docks feeling drowned and exhausted. He was stunned that the city had not been washed away completely. The rain blasted down on him and his team as if someone had simply picked up the ocean, turned it upside down and dropped it on them.

"Holy smokes!" he said in a huff, as he and his team entered the warehouse they called home, "I have never seen anything like this before. If this keeps up, the whole city will be under water."

Looking around slowly he was amazed to see the warehouse had a foot and a half of water covering the floor. All around him, piles of broken crates and shattered machinery littered the floor. It was immediately clear that the structural integrity of the building was perilously close to being compromised.

Skirting along the edge of the wall, he soon found his way blocked by a pile of broken crates. Through that passageway, he knew, was the only safe place on the docks for the cats in the area to live.

"HELLO." he yelled out, "Is anyone still here?" after receiving no response, he tried again, louder. Still no response. Turning to his team he told them to add their voices to his. As a team, they all yelled out to anyone in the building who might hear.

Finally, after their eighth try, Rocky was getting ready to leave, when he heard a soft voice from the other side of the crate barrier.

"Help." came the whispered sound.

"Where are you?" Rocky yelled.

"Just on the other side of the crates, but I can't get past them." came the voice.

"Can you get to the top of the crates, safely?"

"Yes, I think so."

"Great, we'll meet you up there." Rocky instructed.

Rocky was a large and strong cat, but even he knew he would needed help on this project. Turning to his team, he grabbed the two largest, "You two follow me. The rest of you, wait about halfway up the pile. We are going to try and get some of the debris loose from the top, and hand it down to you. For the most part, you can just let it drop from where you will be."

Slowly, and cautiously he began to climb the unstable pile. Twice he slipped and almost knocked down his associates, before gaining secure footing. The other two simply followed his path, allowing him to take the risk.

When they reached the top, they found that a large crate was wedged against the ceiling. He yelled out to the voice on the other side, "Can you hear me?"

"Yes." came the reply.

"We need to get the top crate loose. It is stuck from our side. We will pull, but we need you to push. Can you do that?" Rocky asked.

"Yes... " came a halting voice, "but... I'm not very big."

"No problem..." Rocky chuckled, "we are!"

"Alright, you two get your shoulders against the side of the crate, I'm going to get up top and push from there." Rocky said.

Climbing atop the crate, he wedged his back against the ceiling, and placed his hind legs on the lip of the crate. At the same time, his two partners leaned their shoulders against the side of the crate. Yelling over his shoulder, Rocky asked, "Is everyone ready?"

"Yep", "Oh, yeah" and "Uhhh, I think so." came the response from his two partners and the scared little cat on the other side of the wall.

"Alright, on the count of three, give it all you got." he instructed.

"One... Two... Three."

Giving a great heave, all four of the cats pushed with all their strength, at first they felt nothing, then they heard a creak, and felt a slight movement, "Come on, you guys, it's budging, give it a bit more."

With a growl, they pushed with all their might. For almost half a minute they struggled, but heard only creaking noises from the crate. Then, like a cork from a bottle, the stuck crate came flying out. As it rolled down the pile, the group of cats halfway down guided it past them and let it crash to the floor.

Rocky turned, looked through the hole they had created, and found a tiny beige cat staring at him. Though using the word cat may have been premature, Kitten, was much closer, "Well, well, well... for such a little guy, you did pretty well. My name is Rocky, these are my friends. Are there any more cats on that side."

"No, they headed out when the flood hit, and we got separated. My name is Kale." he said sheepishly.

"Kale? You mean like the vegetable?" Rocky chuckled.

"Yeah, my mom thought it was pretty when she saw a crate of it, and thought it would be a good name." the little guy mumbled.

"Well, I got my name because the field I was born in, was... well... rocky... so, who's to account for parents?" he laughed, "Come on, lets get out of here, we have some friends we are meeting in a safe place."

With little Kale in tow, he climbed down the pile. At the bottom he surveyed his team. They were wet and bedraggled and obviously in need of a rest, "Okay." he said, "We rest for fifteen minutes, then head out."

In a huddle of warm bodies, they gathered together by the door and took a quick cat nap.

Eight

The half mile they had to walk to get above the construction was the hardest work they had ever done. The rain lashed at them seemingly from all directions, and when they reached the first of the two torn up roads, it looked more like a lake, than a road.

Storm turned to CB and shook his head, "CB, how will we ever get through that?" he asked.

"Well, I have an idea, but I am sure you don't want to hear it." he replied.

"Well, unless you have a boat we don't stand much of a chance here." Storm replied.

"Yeah, that's pretty much exactly what I'm thinking."

"WHAT?" Storm screamed, "Have you lost your mind?"

"Well, to be honest, I may have. But here's what I'm thinking. The metal bin has a solid bottom, so it won't take in water. The water is much shallower there on the left, if Keiko stays close to that end, she should be able to float the trash bin across." CB explained.

"That's nuts. Everyone will die."

"Actually, I agree with CB, I was thinking the same thing." Keiko said from behind them, "It's only about thirty feet, they didn't tear up the whole road, just the center. What we will need, is for the cats to be in the water to keep the trash bin upright, and stable. About five on each side should work." Keiko said.

Storm stared at his two friends, and saw the earnestness in their faces, "I can not believe I am agreeing to this. Alright, lets go."

Keiko entered the water first, followed by the ten cats, five on each side of where the trash bin would enter. Slowly, Keiko pulled the bin forward. As the front of the bin hung over the water, a cat swam under the corners and rested the metal on their shoulders. Keiko pulled a little more, and the second set of cats moved under the bin.

Step by step, in this fashion, they maneuvered the bin out over the water. The water was deep, but Keiko found she could touch the bottom, with her head still above the water. The surface area of the bin rested atop the water, and she smoothly guided it across. Storm was stunned when, ten minutes later, they reversed the process and pulled the bin out onto land again.

"Okay, that was amazing." Storm said in awe.

"One down, one to go." CB said as they continued up the hill to the next street.

Arriving at the next street, they found it to be roughly the same set up as the last one, "Okay, team, we've done this before, nice and easy." Keiko said, and again they repeated the process.

They had almost reached the far side, when Max and Norton, the two lead cats lost their hold on the bin and went under the water. The weight of the bin shifted and quickly began nosing down. Storm and CB were the next two cats in line, and try as they might to keep the nose up, they were just not big enough. They slid forward, and tried to reach the front, but could not act fast enough in the water.

Meanwhile, Max and Norton bobbed up from under water and struggled to return to the front of the bin. Swimming as fast as they could, they closed in on the bin quickly.

At the same time, Keiko realized what had happened, and instead of dropping the rope and swimming back to help, she simply stopped. The forward motion of the bin pushed it forward until it rode up on her hips. With her feet firmly planted below her, she was able to hold the bin long enough for Max and Norton to get back in position.

"Everyone okay?" she asked.

"Yeah, I think so." came the joint reply. Slowly, Keiko moved forward again.

When they were finally back on land, Keiko collapsed in a fit of exhaustion, "How about we rest for a bit?" she asked.

"Absolutely." CB replied, "You were amazing."

The team rested for fifteen minutes before resuming their trek up hill. Another ten minutes and they had reached their goal.

* * *

After reaching the road at the top of at the hill and turning toward downtown, CB, Storm, Keiko and the team were able to walk on a flat, straight road for almost two miles. Finally, they found themselves standing at the top of a hill, looking down the street at the west side of the Civic Center.

The road they needed to go down was a gradual decline, as the building remained high up on the hill. It was fairly clear for the first two blocks, then the last four were a raging torrent as water came in from side streets. The water poured into a gully that diverted it away from the building itself, and the Civic Center sat high and relatively safe as the rush of water flowed around it to the right.

Jaffa had been dropped off at his home, and was now safe from harm. While Keiko chatted with the kittens and mothers, calming them, CB and Storm stared down at the road before them.

"We can use the whole road to start, but then we need to move to the left side of the road for that last few blocks. Fortunately, it's a relatively gradual slope, but just in case, lets double check those ropes, I would hate to have them come loose." CB said.

"It might be a good idea for the other cats to follow behind Keiko and the trash bin. We don't want them get run over if it breaks loose." Storm replied.

"Agreed."

A thorough check of the ropes showed them to be solid, but the towel wrapped around the center, which Keiko was using, had been chewed through, and the team took a few minutes to re-wrap it.

When everything was in place, they began the slow march down the hill. The first two blocks blew by with no concerns, but the closer they got to the rushing water the more concern they had. There was very little actual road for them to use, and it was clear that going into the mud on the side of the road was not going to work. As a group, they stopped to talk it over.

"What we really need is someone to keep the back of the bin from pushing me. I have been able, so far, to use my weight to let it rest up against me as I walk, but it is pushing harder, and all the water is going to lessen my stability." Keiko said.

"What if we turned everything around? Instead of pulling the bin, what if you got behind and pushed it. You could use the rope to essentially lower the bin down the road." Storm suggested.

"That might work, let's give it a try." Keiko replied.

Turning the bin around, so the rope was behind it, Keiko picked up the end with her teeth as before, then, stepping inside the loop, she wrapped the rope around her front legs so the rope came out of her mouth, around her shoulders and down between her front legs. This way, she had plenty of control. Walking forward she gave the bin a soft push, and let gravity pull it slowly down the slope and into the torrential waters.

The pull on the bin from the added push of water made Keiko stagger for a few steps, before she lowered her haunches and used her hind legs as a form of brake. Slowly, gradually they moved down the hill, and their goal got closer.

It was as they crossed the second to last street that their world exploded.

Keiko was controlling the descent, keeping it slow and steady, when suddenly the rushing water swept her feet from under her. As if in slow motion, she felt herself fall, and in a daze she saw the rope come loose, fly around her legs and get yanked out of her mouth.

Keiko landed on her back and the bin, filled with kittens and nursing mothers, went into free fall, hurling itself down the road.

* * *

Storm watched in horror as Keiko's legs flew out from under her. In an instant she was in the air, and the rope was flying free. He saw the big dog land squarely on her back and begin sliding down the hill. He saw her vainly trying to regain her footing and rush toward the runaway trash bin.

In front of him, the bin was rapidly picking up speed. Without thinking, he turned and ran toward the bin. He had only run a few feet, when the water pushed his legs away from him and he was suddenly sliding more than running. Panic began to set in as he found himself hurling out of control through the rushing water, and toward the metal bin.

Just when he thought there was no way he could regain control, he felt his paws touch a bit of solid ground. Using that brief respite, and all of his speed and agility, he spun around, settled his hind legs under him and jumped with all his strength.

* * *

CB, like the others, was horrified by the sight. He was moving before the thought even crossed his mind what would happen if they could not stop the runaway bin.

He was on the same side of the bin that Keiko and Storm were on, but on a relatively dry patch of land. He saw Keiko struggle to her feet and start running toward the bin, at the same time that Storm managed to get his feet under him.

Without thought or communication, CB followed his two friends and jumped at exactly the same second, heading at the side of the rushing bin.

* * *

As Keiko felt her feet touch solid ground beneath her, she saw Storm struggling to gain his footing at the same time. Knowing that if she got in front of the bin, she would be crushed by its weight and speed, she took three long strides and jumped with all her strength.

From the corner of her eye she saw Storm jump at the same time, and just past him, she saw the big, charcoal grey missile of CB flying through the air in the same arc.

Like a giant, three part battering ram, the weight of two large cats and a giant dog hit the side of the bin at exactly the same time. They seemed to know that there was no way to stop the bin, but their combined weight was enough to knock it off course and send it sliding into the mud. As the first set of wheels hit dirt, combined with the weight of the three animals pushing it, the entire bin came to a halt and flew over onto its side.

Like a projectile from a cannon, cats and kittens blew out of the toppled bin and landed in a heap on a patch of grass.

Nine

CB, Keiko and the rest of the cats rushed over to where the kittens and mothers had landed, and were beginning to assess the situation, when they suddenly heard the sound of uncontrolled laughter coming from Storm, behind them. Anger flared instantly in CB and he spun to face Storm.

"Really, Storm!!" he yelled, "I fail to see what you find so hilarious about this situation."

Storm, quite too uncontrolled in his laughter, could not respond. Raising his right front paw, he simply pointed.

CB turned to face the direction Storm was pointing, and after taking a split second to register what Storm was pointing at, he too burst out laughing.

It turned out that they had landed in a tuft of grass on the edge of the parking lot for the Civic Center. Twenty five feet away, sitting on his haunches before an open air vent was Herbie. He had his front paws in front of his mouth, his eyes were bugged out and he had a look of abject terror on his face. Clearly, he had witnessed the whole scene with the trash bin as it had played out.

In seconds, the entire group had joined the laughter as they took in the look on Herbie's face, and absorbed the relief that they had reached safety.

When the laughter finally died down, CB apologized to Storm for yelling at him, and turned to the rest of the group.

"Alright, all of you. It's great to be here safely, but it is still pouring down rain, and I'm tired of being cold and wet. Everyone grab a kitten by the scruff of the neck, and get inside and warm."

Several of the kittens were placed on Keiko's back and were given a special ride to their new home. Max and Norton each grabbed a kitten, as did Storm and CB. When they arrived, and everyone was heading inside, CB handed his kitten over to its mother and turned to Keiko.

"Once again, the cats owe you their lives. But not just theirs, the lives of the mothers and kittens, as well. We can never repay you." he said sincerely.

"I am only glad I could be there to help. You're my family, it's all I can do." Keiko replied softly.

"Well, the family fortune is ours then. We can never thank you enough. However, it's going to be light soon, you better get back home. Stay safe, old friend, avoid the flooded areas." CB said.

"No worries, I have a route planned out." the big Akita replied.

As she turned to leave, she saw Storm come up in front her. As usual, he didn't say a word, he simply laid his forehead against hers and held it there for a moment. No words were needed, they had said it all.

* * *

Ten minutes later the team was gathered in the large hall of the Civic Center. As grooming and drying commenced for some, others, who had been there for a while, went out in search of mice and rats for food.

CB found a warm and quiet spot below one of the skylights and set up a nursery for the kittens and mothers, while Storm helped the other cats find tarps and old sheets for bedding. Sleep would come easy for the cats that night.

Looking around, Storm noticed that Rocky was missing, as was the rest of his team. In a corner, he saw Herbie and CB talking quietly with Max and Norton, and quickly made his way over.

"Any word on Rocky?" he asked.

"No, we were just talking about that. They were headed into the worst of the flooding. We have placed a sentry at the opening to the entrance to guide them in when they get here." the concern in CB's voice was palpable.

"Well, I, for one, will not rest until they are here and everyone is accounted for." Storm said.

"Yeah, none of us will." CB and Herbie said in unison.

For the next hour, the cats kept themselves busy eating and planning. They knew they were safe for a while, there were no immediate plans to raze the building that they knew of, and it would take weeks before the city clean up reached the point where someone would worry about the old Civic Center, yet they knew that it was only a short term fix to a long term problem.

The cat leadership worked on ideas for a new home. Obviously they could not go back to the alley, that was destroyed. Going to one of the farms would be too far away, as were the docks. They needed to be close to the work they did. There were too many problems to be solved, and only their team could solve them.

"I don't know." CB sighed. "And I have a feeling we won't figure it out tonight."

"Good, because I would be seriously hacked off if you made that decision without me." came a voice from behind them.

Herbie was the first to jump up and run to the new voice. "Rocky, you made it."

"Well, of course we did, who was going to stop us?" he said with a laugh.

"Welcome to our... well, let's call it our 'temporary home'." CB laughed.

"We'll get settled in a bit, but first let me introduce you to our newest member. Everyone, this is Kale. Kale... this is everyone." Rocky said with a smile.

Kale was welcomed warmly by the team and was given a home with the adolescent cats. Meanwhile, Rocky filled them in on the adventure of the docks.

"As far as I know all the cats are safe, but it's hard to know for certain. The docks are a mess. Herbie and I will have our hands full down there after everyone returns, and the humans start cleaning up." he sighed, "I have a feeling that Kale may be of some assistance there. He is quiet, and a bit shy, but he reminds me a lot of Jaffa, and we could use a brain like that down on the docks."

"You'll do a great job raising him, I am certain." Storm said. He had the world of respect for the team of leaders CB had developed, and was not too shy to let them know.

"In the meantime, what the heck are we going to do for a home?" CB asked, almost to himself.

"I don't know, CB." Storm said, "But that is a decision for another night."

The Cat Burglar:
A Christmas Carol

One

As the sun set outside the Civic Center, a cool dampness settled on the large, main hall. An eerie orange light flowed down from the sky light far over the heads of the cats scattered around the main exhibit floor. Some were sleeping, but since cats are, as nature designed them, crepuscular, they are always most active at dawn and dusk.

With a sigh of relief, CB looked around at the cats he called his friends. They were a large group now, really too large. With all the kittens, they numbered seventy-two. It was time to thin out his team. Small groups of cats can hide easily, seventy-two cannot.

Life in the Civic Center had proven to be a good choice. Not that they had much of an option, it was either there or dead. Not much of a choice as far as he was concerned. But their safety here was limited. They had already had to hide from the human workers who came to inspect the building after the flood, twice. He did not relish having to do so again. It was just too hard to move the kittens, and some of the adolescents were still learning when it was appropriate to play, and when it wasn't. Six had almost been caught the last time the workers came though.

CB sighed. So far, the humans did not know they were there. Another stunt like the adolescents played and their safety was over. He needed to find a new home for the cats, and he needed to split them up... and he need to do it soon. With winter only a few weeks away, he could not afford to wait much longer. They needed to be in their new home, and safe, before the first snowfall hit.

Part of that was easy. A dozen of the cats would return to the docks, under the watchful eyes of Rocky and Herbie. Fifteen of the cats had decided to join Ben at the farm and start training to create a new clan out there. But that still left CB with forty-five cats. And, twenty of them were barely walking.

Yawning and stretching to loosen his stiff muscles, CB slowly stood and began a stroll around the main hall. He stopped by the nursery and was greeted by twenty of the cutest kittens he had ever laid eyes on, "Yeah, but you say that about every fresh batch of kittens." he said to himself, and chuckled.

Even in the four days since the rain had stopped, eleven days after it began, he could see that the kittens had grown. Awkward little balls of fluff were becoming coordinated in their movements, and their soft little mews were growing deeper. Another week or two and they may be able to travel on their own. But CB knew they didn't have that long. They needed a new home now, not in two weeks.

"You have that contemplative, worried look on your face again, old man." a voice said behind him. Without even turning to look, he smiled at the voice. Storm had become his closest friend, and his strongest leader. Where CB was serious, Storm was a joker. Where CB was a worrier, Storm took life as it came. But inside that rash body, was a calculating brain unlike any he had ever seen before. Sure, Jaffa may be technically smarter, but Storm was very close behind, and leaps and bounds beyond Jaffa in street smarts.

As CB turned around he saw that Storm was flanked by Rocky, Herbie, Max, Norton, Jaffa, Marti and Meow Meow. His entire leadership team.

"Aha, so the gangs all here, what is this, a coup?" CB said with a laugh.

"Hardly! No one could do your job, nor would they want to." Storm said, "What we are, or hope to be, is the solution to all your worries."

"Really? And how do you plan to do that?" CB chuckled.

"By providing you with not one, but two safe new places for the cats to live." Storm said with a grin.

CB felt his heart begin beating faster. This was more than he could hope for. But, for all Storm's playfulness, practical jokes were not his forte. Storm may be playful, but he was also deathly serious about the safety of the clan.

"Alright, lay it on me." CB chuckled.

"Oh, no. Not me... this is Jaffa's find, not mine." he said with a laugh, "Go ahead, Jaffa, lay it on him."

As the leadership team chuckled, Jaffa donned his sheepish look, "Yeah, well, it might not be much, but, well, I have an idea." he mumbled.

"Really, Jaffa, after all this time, I cannot believe you are still so nervous around CB. Or Tyler, if you want to be less formal." Rocky said with a laugh. Rocky was one of the oldest of the cats, and as tough as he was big. But not far below the surface lay one of the biggest hearts, and one of the kindest and most caring cats, that Jaffa had ever met.

"Yeah, well... respect is earned. And CB has earned it." Jaffa replied sheepishly.

"And the rest of us haven't, is that what you're saying?" Rocky chuckled.

" WHAT... NO... that's not what I mean." Jaffa stammered.

"Jaffa, relax... I'm only joking. Jeesh, for a smart cat, you have a lot to learn about kidding around." Rocky laughed.

"Sorry, I'm working on that, but it would have helped if I were raised around other cats." he smiled, knowing the other cat was only being friendly, "Anyway, on my way back to The Heights last night when I left here, I decided to take a different route. Instead of going down the hill, over to Jones and back up to The Heights, I decided to go up instead. But, I didn't go as far up as you folks did when you came here, I only went up three blocks, then cut over and continued heading south from there. About half way between here and The Heights, I found a set of old buildings that the humans had used before the flood, but it's really obvious they aren't going to use them again." Jaffa stopped and took a deep breath. Looking around him, he saw dubious looks on the team's faces.

"Ummm, no disrespect, young man," Herbie said softly, "but how could you possibly tell from one look that the humans weren't coming back?"

"Oh... sorry... I meant to explain that. Well, remember in our old alley, there were orange pieces of paper hanging on a bunch of the windows?" he asked, and received a group nod in reply, "Well, of course none of us can read the human writing, but the biggest word across the top of those pages was the same as I saw on the new set of buildings.

"I'm thinking that word is what we would call 'condemned'. We don't go near places we feel are condemned, and I don't think the humans do either. These new buildings are much more solid than the other buildings in town that were destroyed by the flood. I figure, if they are going to bother taking buildings down eventually because they are condemned, then they are going to go after the more severe buildings first. It will be years, maybe decades before the ones I found are touched." Jaffa finished.

Storm stared at Jaffa. This was the second time he had heard this story from him and he was no less amazed this time than he was the first, "Wow!" he said quietly to Jaffa, "You are one scary smart cat. Go ahead, tell him the rest."

"Oh, yeah. There's another set of buildings, very similar to the first set, about a mile and a half further on, just on the far edge of The Heights. Both are centrally located, both are well sheltered, both have workable alleys and all of the buildings seem solid enough that we could actually live in them, rather than out in the alley like we did before."

Without a seconds hesitation, CB replied, "Show me!" and headed toward the exit.

Two

Three days later was moving day. The alleys Jaffa had found were not just perfect, they were leaps and bounds beyond perfect. CB could easily split his clan, creating two solid groups a mile and a half apart. They could patrol different parts of town much more smoothly, and still come together as a team in a very short time if needed.

CB would reside in the eastern alley with ten of his strongest leaders, the mothers and the kits. Max and Norton would manage the western alley.

Rocky and Herbie would return to the docks with their team. Meow Meow and the new lieutenant, Kale, would join them.

Storm would remain in the alley with CB, helping to look after the youngest of the team, and would be promoted to coordinator of the teams. He would roam between the four teams (including the team at Ben's farm) and keep track of the day to day activities. For the first time ever, CB and his teams could watch the entire city, rather than just parts of it, "Now," he said to himself, "we can really get some work done."

The first, and most important issue, were the kittens. They could all walk by now, but this distance was way beyond them. He had to get them all to the new site safely. He thought about Keiko and the trash bin, then laughed at his own silliness. Once with that trick was more than enough.

"Alright, everyone, listen up." he yelled to the group of cats in the main hall, "There are twenty kittens, and fifty-two adults. For every kitten, there is a scruff, for every scruff, I want a mouth! I want all of the big males to grab a kitten by the scruff and head out. Mothers, you follow them. Everyone else, find the blankets, towels and anything else you can carry that you think will be helpful, and head on out. The new alley and buildings have tons of debris, so we will find much of what we need when we get there." he instructed.

As he stepped out of the hatch into the cool, dark night, he saw Storm waiting for him, "Quite a beautiful night, is it not?" Storm said quietly.

"Why, yes, it is." CB replied. He knew that tone in Storm's voice, and the look in his eye, "What are you up to, Storm."

"Do I look like I'm up to something?" Storm asked with feigned shock.

"Well, as the old saying goes, Storm, 'when you look like your up to nothing... you're up to something!'" CB laughed.

"Well, now that you mention it, I just thought you might enjoy a bit of female companionship during the trip to your new home." Storm said with a grin, and stepped aside to reveal a stunningly beautiful, solid white Persian cat.

"PARADISE!!!" CB yelled, "What are you doing here? You can't be away from your home, your humans will be frantic... or stroke... or something."

"My humans are away for a few hours, and Storm thought I would like to accompany you to your new home. He was, of course, correct... though, I am not sure you should admit that to him, he's kind of full of himself, already." Paradise said with a playful poke in Storm's ribs. It was Storm who had saved her when she was kidnapped, a debt she could never repay. Her admiration for her little friend knew no bounds.

"Yeah, well, if you two love birds will excuse me, I have organizing to do." Storm said as he moved off.

"He's a great friend to you, you do realize that, don't you?" Paradise said to CB when Storm had moved off.

"Oh, yeah. There has never been a better friend in my life than Storm. Probably never will be either." CB said in all earnestness.

"Well, don't sell yourself short, you are as good a friend to him as he is to you."

"Oh, don't I know it. Two peas in a pod, the two of us. I only wish we could find a new female for him to hook up with, he was quite devastated by what happened to Ginka." CB said softly. Ginka was Marti's sister, and Storm's first true love. She had taken ill earlier in the Fall, and her humans had no choice but to put her down. It was a remarkably sad time, and all the more so for her humans. According to Marti, they were still mourning the loss.

"Well, all things come with time, big boy." Paradise winked.

CB burst out laughing, "You have a plan, don't you." CB asked.

"No, I have an idea, they are two different things. You see, as you know, your clan gained a few new cats who were displaced from their homes during the flood. Many of them are female. Storm is a great cat… strong, smart, kind, funny, super handsome… the females will flock to him as soon as everything is settled again.

"Come on, I only have a couple hours before my humans return, and someone has to hold the screen open, like Storm did, so I can get back in." Paradise said with a laugh, and the two old lovers moved off in search of their team.

Three

Three weeks after settling into their new homes, the cats were slowly becoming acclimated. Cats, by their nature, abhor change. And this, had been change at the most ridiculous level.

A nursery had been built in the new building, as well as a dormitory of sorts for the adolescents. The older cats had resumed their lessons with the younger cats, and order was being restored. The building in the second alley was completed, and plans were in the works for a nursery there as well. They were just entering Winter, but Spring wouldn't be far behind, and Spring always meant more kittens.

As he settled himself into an old leather couch which had been left behind, and which had become his new home-within-his-home, CB looked out the window at a raging snowstorm. Winters were long in the city, but the cats were well prepared. At least this year they could be indoor and out of the cold and wind.

CB looked toward the door and saw Storm gazing out at the town in the distance. Jumping off the couch, CB strolled over to his friend and said quietly, "Something on your mind, Storm?"

"Yeah, I guess there is. Look out at the town, CB. All the human houses and buildings. They're all decorated with lights and colorful ribbons. I remember seeing this last year, too, but I was never able to figure it out. Why do they do that at this time of year? And while we're at it, what's with all the humans downtown dressed in red suits and white beards, ringing bells?" Storm asked.

"Those are great questions, Storm. Even in all my years I have never been able to understand this. Every year, right about the end of Fall, or start of Winter, the humans decorate the town and all the guys in red suits show up. I don't get it. But, I have also noticed that the humans seem kinder and more helpful at this time than at any other time during the year. Like, maybe they are reviewing their years and trying to be nicer. I don't know..." CB said with a shake of his head.

"Who's to explain humans?" Storm said with a chuckle, "But it does make you think, doesn't it. I mean, we spend all year trying to help others, but there's something to be said about stepping back once a year and looking at things fresh to see if maybe something needs to be revisited and revised."

"Hmmm... interesting comments, Storm. I think I agree with you, but I get a feeling that you have something specific in mind." CB said.

"Well, yeah, I guess I do." Storm said, still staring out into the distance, "Overall, I really think we did a great job this year... but, I am still concerned that we didn't do the right thing out at the farm."

CB sighed and settled down next to his friend, "Emily!!", he said softly.

"Yeah." Storm agreed, "I know we did what we could, based upon what we knew at the time, but I just can't be comfortable with the outcome. It almost seems that we caused more problems than we solved."

"I can't disagree at all, Storm. We need to remember that Emily gave us little choice at the time, but we definitely could have been more creative."

As the two friends stared out at the lights of the city below them, and contemplated what to do, they heard a commotion by the entrance to the alley, and were shocked by the sound of barking mixed in. Glancing over at Storm, CB said, "That sounds like Korkie."

"What the heck is he doing here?" Storm asked as the two of them jumped up and ran to the entrance to the alley. When they arrived, they found the old cocker spaniel/poodle mix surrounded by hissing cats.

"Cats, back off. He's a friend." Storm yelled.

As the cats ran off, CB and Storm turned to their old friend.

"Hi CB, hi Storm. Oh, wait, sorry CB, do you actually prefer Tyler, now? I can never remember what to call you." Korkie said with a chuckle.

"No worries, old friend, I seem to be confusing a lot of the animals with that nowadays." CB laughed, "Either one is fine."

"Oh, good, that will make it easier. This looks like a nice new home for you, is it working out well?"

"Better than we ever expected. And it helps a lot that we have two alleys now so we can cover more territory." Storm answered.

"That's really great. I've been meaning to come up and see the new place, but its kind of hard to get away from the farm."

"Well, you are always welcome, would you like a tour?" CB asked.

"I'd love one. Thanks. Oh, wait, we can't... there's a problem out at the farm, we need to hurry back." Korkie said, "Gosh, my memory sure isn't what it used to be."

"Problem, what problem?" CB asked in a rush.

"Well, some humans were driving around the corner down the road from the farms, and slid on the snow. They weren't really hurt much, and they got the wreck cleaned up, but apparently they had some puppies in the car that ran away during the chaos. The humans searched all day, but could not find them."

"What about Ben and the cats, couldn't they help?" Storm asked with frustration clear in his voice. What good was it to have a team out there, if they needed help with such simple issues as finding a couple puppies.

"Oh, heck, the cats were great, they searched all day, but apparently the little guys got into the woods, and... well, cats aren't really trackers like dogs are. Hunter, Jackson and I tried, but we must be getting old, and can't get the scent." Korkie said sheepishly, "Sorry."

"Not to worry, my friend, none of us are as young as we used to be." CB said, "Sounds like we need to get some help from Keiko. Storm, would you mind getting her and meeting us at the farm?"

"Sure, be glad to. Ummm, sorry for my frustration a moment ago. It's been a long couple weeks." Storm mumbled.

As the three friends laughed, Storm ran off to meet get the biggest dog in town.

Four

An hour later CB, Storm, Keiko and Korkie all stood inside the barn with Ben and the other cats. Keiko had been brought up to speed with the situation and was weighing their options.

"We need to hurry, this storm is picking up, and it has already been snowing most of the day. It's also getting colder as the day goes on. Hopefully, the little guys have found a a spot to hide, which is out of the wind and snow, but time is rushing by and they could be in trouble." the big Akita said.

"What can we do? We cats aren't trackers like you dogs." Ben asked.

"Yeah, and not all of us dogs are trackers either. My breed are protectors, not trackers. We have good noses, but we're all about strength and cunning. We need a tracker." saying this she looked over at CB and held her breath. She knew what she was suggesting, and the problems of the past.

"Look, I know where you are leading, Keiko, but this is not the time for taking chances." CB said softly.

"No, CB, this is exactly the time for chances." Storm said, "This is, quite literally, what she was bred for."

"I know, but she's not exactly reliable is she? We need cool, calm thinking, not high strung running around." CB said.

"Look, I agree, but this may be the time for Emily to find out what she's made of." Keiko said, "This could be her time."

"Risking the lives of the the pups, may not be the right time to test her mettle."

"Or, it may be the perfect time." Ben replied.

CB sighed and took a deep breath, "Alright, let's get moving then. We may be running out of time. Where is she anyway? I haven't heard or seen her?"

"Well," Korkie said, "that's another problem. She's in the house and our humans have been gone all day."

"Then let's get her out of there." Storm said, and started toward the other farm.

"Storm, wait." Ben said, "We can't just break the door down."

"Why not?" Storm replied.

"Well, for two reasons. One, because we have no way of knowing that she will understand if we yell to her from outside the house, and if we break in and surprise her, someone could get hurt. And two... because her humans just got home, and she will be out in the yard in a matter of minutes anyway." Ben said, as the whole group started laughing.

"Ah, well in that case, who's up for a stroll and a chat?" Storm laughed.

* * *

As the team arrived at the other farm, Emily came flying out the back door. She was anxious and running around, but CB noticed that the last few months seemed to have calmed her some.

"What are all of you doing here?" Emily asked as she ran around the team.

CB stepped forward and explained the situation. "Oh, my gosh," Emily said, "we need to find them. Where do we start?"

"Well, that's the problem," Storm replied, "we know where they went into the forest, but we can't find their scent after that. All we cats can smell is the heavy scent of pine. We need a sharper nose."

"I have that. Look, guys, I know I'm high strung, and hard to deal with, but you taught me a lot about myself over the past few months. I understand that helping others is much more important than just helping myself, now. I can do this, it is what I was bred for. Show me where they went in." Emily said as honestly as she could.

Keiko led her over to where the pups had entered the forest, and leaned over to whisper in her ear, "Emily, this is what you were born to do. None of the rest of us can find these pups. The snow is coming down harder and the wind is getting worse, this is going to be very dangerous. But, you can do this."

"Thanks," the little dog said, "I appreciate your support. I know I haven't earned anyone's trust yet, and that's my fault. But, those pups need help, and that's what's most important. I'll be careful, but I'll find them and bring them here safely."

The little dog, with the spring in her step jumped up and touched noses with the giant Akita, then for the first time anyone had ever seen, she just stopped, concentrated on the task and slowly started sniffing the ground, finding the scent almost immediately.

"Really, you guys can't smell this... heck, the scent is screaming at me." Emily said with a laugh, and was pleased to see the others laugh with her. Then, focusing

on her job, she slid into the forest and disappeared from
the site of the team.

Five

While the trees helped block some of the snow and cold, Emily continued to shiver as the biting storm blew the snow around the woods. The snow was less deep inside the tree line, but still rose almost to Emily's knees.

For a moment, Emily stopped and looked around her. There was no point of reference for her to follow. No paw prints, no sounds of barking or whining, not even something simple like a shivering puppy standing in a clearing waiting for her to find them, "How," she asked herself, "can I ever accomplish this? What was I thinking?"

For the first time since she agreed to do this, Emily was overwhelmed with doubt. If she failed, these pups would die. She had never done anything to help others, and her first big try risked not only her life, but the lives of three small pups as well.

"I can't do this." she said out loud, and started to turn back. Then she stopped again, "No, I can do this. I must do this." she said to herself. With that, she turned back to the woods.

"Okay, let's go." she said. Sniffing the air around her she found nothing on the air to help her, "Well, it has been four hours, they could have travelled quite a distance by now." a blast of bitter cold air rushed in at her and she turned away to avoid the worst of it, "If I were a pup, being blasted by frigid air, and needing to find shelter, where would I go?"

Looking around she saw a clump of small bushes to her left and strolled in that direction. At the base of a small yew, he found a spot of urine, "Well, at least your mom taught you to how to lift your leg when you go." she laughed aloud.

This was her first big hint, and more importantly, she now had a stronger scent to follow. Reaching out with her left paw she scooped a small amount of the urine and rubbed it on her right rear leg. With that, she could refresh her memory of the scent whenever she needed to, but it would be behind her, so she could differentiate between what she was seeking, and what she had already smelled.

Emily looked longingly behind her at the passage between the trees which would send her back to the blissful ignorance of running around her yard antagonizing the other animals. All she had to do was take a few steps and head back to her warm house. With a shake of her head, she turned back to the small bush with the scent mark. No, she thought to herself, those puppies need me.

Starting at the small bush, she began making a close circuit of it, only to find that she was still too close to the scent marking. Stepping back, she began making slow circuits of the bush. She needed to get far enough away that she could smell the scent, without being overwhelmed.

On her fourth trip around the bush, and about fifteen feet away from the urine scent, she finally found what she needed. The scent of puppies, not urine. Three puppies, actually. Two female, one male. She was on the north side of the bush, and the puppies appeared to have headed off in that direction. Time to go, she thought. Besides, she was freezing to death, she needed to move.

Six

CB paced back and forth before the trees where Emily entered the forest. He was freezing, and shivering, and ice was caked to his fur. Yet, he couldn't leave. He had never had a problem putting himself in danger to help, others, but he hated sending others in.

And now, it was Emily. He truly liked Emily, but knew from experience that she was high strung and often made decisions without thinking them through. Not really a problem day to day, but dangerous beyond words when others lives were on the line.

From the corner of his eye he saw Storm sitting by the opening in the trees. Unlike CB, Storm sat quietly, huddled in a snow covered ball, staring into the forest. With a sigh and a chuckle, CB sidled over to his best friend.

"I know, Storm. I'm worried about her too." he said when he reached Storm's side.

Storm never moved as he responded, "It's cold, Tyler, and her fur isn't as thick as ours. She's also not used to being outside like we are."

"I know, Storm, I have the same concerns. And, she's headstrong, it will be hard for her to focus on her current job. Yet, and I know I have never been a huge supporter of her, I think there may be more to her than I gave her credit for." CB said calmly.

"I agree, CB. This is her watershed moment. Who she is will be determined tonight. I just wish there weren't the lives of other animals in the balance."

"I know, and I agree. We are in for a long night, you should head in and warm up."

"Not a chance. I will be right here until someone walks out of that forest." Storm said, finally looking at CB.

"Well, then, move over and make room for another body, because I'm not going anywhere either."

With a short laugh, the two friends huddled together by the trees, "Ummm... you do know that you are completely covered in snow, don't you?" CB said with a laugh.

"Oh, not for long." Storm said as he jumped up and shook the snow all over CB. And, for the next couple minutes, the two old friends warmed themselves with play fighting.

Seven

Starting off at a slow jog Emily followed the track for the next half hour. The scent was very faint. The pups had left this area a long time ago, and the scent was fading.

The problem, she knew clearly, was that she was rapidly freezing to death, and she seriously needed to find some form of shelter. And, if she needed shelter, then the pups had to be in desperate need.

With her nose inches from the snow, and often buried deep in the snow, she kept following what she could find of the scent. The trail was making her insane. Typical of puppies, they were roaming all over the place. North, south, east, back north, south again, it was maddening.

Then, with a burst of hysterical laughter, she had the clearest revelation of her life, "Oh... My... Goodness!!!" she screamed out loud, "THIS, is what CB, Storm and the rest of the animals thought of me!!! No wonder they made that deal with the rats and did what they did. They probably should have just killed me outright!"

With that laugh, she started off again. The wind and snow continued to buffet her, and she could feel her limbs, and her mind, beginning to freeze. She had to find the pups, and shelter, soon or frozen corpses are all that would be left of her and the pups.

* * *

Emily had travelled a mile into the forest, when suddenly she realized she was losing the scent. In a moment of panic, she ran around in circles trying to find the scent again. She retraced her trail, but no matter what she did, she was hopelessly lost. The trail was gone.

With a deep sigh, she realized she had failed. She had lost the pups, she had lost the trail, and the reality was, she had lost her last ounce of energy. She was freezing to death, probably didn't have more than a few minutes left, and the most important job of her life was a lost cause.

Tears rolled down her frosted cheeks as she realized it was all over. She could not help any more, and the frustration made her want to scream. But even that wouldn't work. Her mouth and throat were so cold, she couldn't speak any longer.

As she lay in a huddle, wallowing in her frustration, her eyes began to close and she knew she had only moments left.

It was then, as the last of her energy faded and her life was slipping away, that she heard footsteps approaching.

For a moment, she thought she must be hallucinating. Surely, there wasn't anyone around. She was in the middle of a forest, in a blizzard, freezing to death... there were no humans around. Yet, the steady crunch of footsteps continued. Shaking the cobwebs from her brain, and the snow from her coat, she looked over her shoulder to find the strangest site she could imagine.

There, standing not two feet from her was the largest human Emily had ever seen. Easily six feet four inches tall, and weighing somewhere in the vicinity of 400 pounds, the man sported a gigantic white beard and a red fur suit with white trim.

Emily, as one would expect, burst out laughing. So this is the way her hallucination would take her into oblivion. With some bizarre fantasy about that crazy red suited guy that she had seen in town when her humans took her for a drive. She had no idea who the character was, but it must have made some impression in her mind, if this is what she dreamt up for her last vision.

"Well, little one, you seem to be a bit lost." the giant human said. His voice was deep and seemed to fill the whole forest with it's depth.

Emily stared at the apparition in front of her. Her reality was slipping away, and she felt a tear slide down her cheek.

"No worries, little one." the big man continued, "Everyone gets lost from time to time."

Emily just stared as the last of her thoughts flooded through her mind, "I know I'm lost." she said quietly, "But I don't know what to do."

"Well, little one, things aren't completely lost yet."

"But how can't they be lost?" Emily said through her tears, "I lost the scent of the pups and I can't find them. And now, I just can't seem to find the energy to keep looking. The pups are going to die and I can't help them. I failed, and the reality is, that's what everyone expected." Emily cried.

"Nothing can be truly lost while there's still hope, little one."

"But how can there be hope?"

"Well, little one, there can always be hope if you only believe." the giant red man chuckled, "Look, Emily, CB and Storm doubted you because you didn't give them a reason to believe in you. And why would they, when you didn't believe in yourself."

"But I didn't really know, did I?" Emily cried

"Perhaps not. And more importantly, you didn't allow those who could help you to know either. Tyler and Storm tried to do the best with what they had, but they had no way of knowing what else to do. Now they have taken the chance on you and have given you a second chance. What are you going to do with it?"

"What can I do?" Emily sniffled.

"Well, little one, you can start by getting into that little cave over there and warm up." Emily looked in the direction he was pointing and saw a small opening in the hill behind them.

"Emily," the man in red said softly, "you are a great dog. But you need to believe in yourself. Be patient, be calm and listen. CB, Storm, Keiko and the other animals will be great teachers for you. You have a lot of great times ahead of you. But, for now, you have work to do, and it needs to start with getting out of this storm... and taking care of some pups."

"But I can't find the pups." Emily yelled. And that's when she heard a reply. A soft whimper in the direction of the small cave. With a laugh she realized the pups were smarter than she was, they had found shelter. She turned to thank the man in the red suit, but he was gone. All that remained of the man in red, was the crumpled snow where his feet had trampled it.

In a rush Emily ran over to the small cave and squeezed herself in. There, she found the three pups. They were together in a corner, but not really together. She walked over them and introduced herself, "Hi, my name is Emily. I came to take you back to your humans. But first, I think we need to get some rest, and see if we can warm each other up."

The pups looked at her and smiled, feeling some safety for the first time, "Okay the three of you, get together. Your bodies will generate heat, and if you huddle together, you can share that. And, since I am bigger than you, adding my warmth should help all of us." curling up with them, she felt them begin to relax, and for the next hour they all took a long nap, relishing the warmth they were all generating.

Eight

"That's it, I'm going in." Storm said. It had been just over four hours since Emily had entered the forest,

"Not without me, you're not." CB replied as the two old friends jumped up and started shaking the snow off their coats. It took a few minutes to get their limbs moving again after being huddled in the cold for so long.

As they started walking toward the entrance between the trees, they saw Keiko come strolling over. "Where do you two think you're going?" she asked.

"We're going in to get Emily. She's been in there much too long and has to be frozen by now. She needs our help." CB replied.

"Well, you're not going in without me!" she replied.

"Keiko, what are you even doing here, you need to get back home before your human finds out you're missing and has a heart attack worrying about you." Storm chided

"My human is away from home for 10 hours every day. It has currently been seven and a half hours since she left, so I have two and a half hours left. It takes less than an hour to get home, so I have an hour and a half to help you search."

"Nice calculations, you sounded like Jaffa for a second there." Storm said with sarcasm dripping.

"Not bad, at least I sounded like one of the smartest cats!" Keiko shot back. The big dog and the little cat looked at each other for a moment, before they both burst out laughing.

"What am I going to do with the two of you?" CB said with a smile, "Okay, let's get going."

As they moved toward the entrance to the forest, they saw a slight movement in the snow. Not much, more like a brief change in the breeze. They stopped and looked at each other.

"Do you hear…" Keiko started.

"What the heck…" Storm replied.

"Is that… singing?" CB asked.

The three old friends looked at each other in wonder. They must have frozen their brains after all this time outside. Then, from out of the swirling snow, the saw the most wondrous site.

* * *

Keiko stopped short when she looked into the forest, and thought she had lost her mind. Maybe this is what a hallucination looks like. Coming towards her from out of the snow, she saw what appeared to be a small dog, but it was standing on it's hind legs, bouncing up and down and waving its front legs, while singing at the top of its voice.

* * *

Storm stared at the vision in front of him and did what he does best… burst out laughing. The site in front of him reminded him of the day he had accidentally eaten a bad piece of chicken and had gotten so sick that he couldn't think straight. It was like a vision out of some crazy dream. Surely, he thought, his brain synapses had ceased firing correctly and he had frozen to death a while ago.

*　*　*

CB saw Keiko stop short in wonder, and heard a peal of laughter come from Storm before he got between them and could see what they saw. His first reaction was the same as Keiko's, but seconds later he was emulating Storm, as tears of laughter rolled down his cheeks.

Coming toward them was what appeared to be Emily. She was covered in snow and ice so thick that she looked half again her regular size. She was hopping on her hind legs, flailing her front legs like she was leading a band. All the while, she was singing, as loudly as she could, some distinctly off key tune he had never heard before.

Behind her, also hopping along on their hind legs to the best of their ability, and singing, if possible, even more out of tune, were three very frozen looking puppies.

Nine

When Emily woke in the small cave, she was still shivering with cold. Her body heat was still too low, and she was sure the temps of the pups were also too low. But, she did feel somewhat better.

Rousing the pups, she did a quick check to make sure they were okay, "Okay, all of you, what are your names?" she asked.

"Umm..." the male said, "we don't have names yet, our mom wanted to wait until we got to our humans home, so we learned what they called us and didn't have to make a change."

"Well, that's an interesting approach. How about I call you "one", "two" and "three", just so we know who we're talking to?" Emily chuckled.

"Okay... do you want me to be One?" the little male asked.

"Yep. And your sister is Two, and your other sister is Three. Now, I know you are cold, and you did a great job of finding shelter, but we need to get out of here. We need to get you to my farm, where you can get warm and get some food and water." Emily said.

"But, the storm is really bad out there." Two said with a quiver in her voice. The pups were trying to sound strong, but she could tell they were scared.

"I know, and you guys have done great so far. But, if we stay here we will either freeze to death or starve to death in a couple hours. We only have about a mile and a half to go. With little legs like ours, that's going to take us about an hour. So, here's what I want to do. I want us to move very quickly, but not run. We will use up all of our energy if we go too fast. We need a steady pace. Does that make sense?"

"Yep." all three of the pups said.

"Okay, here's what we're going to do. Once we get out of the cave, it will be hard to see each other through all the blowing snow. So, I want you to keep your eyes and ears on me at all times. I will make sure you can see and hear me, just follow as close as you can."

"Okay, when do you want to go?" came the response.

"Now." Emily said, "Everyone follow me, and again, make sure you stay close."

Stepping out of the cave, the four dogs were hit by a blast of wind and snow. The cold bit through them, and the little pups froze in place. No, no, no, Emily thought, that won't work, "Guys, you need to follow me, we can't stay here. I tell you what we're going to do. I am going to sing a song. One, you repeat it as soon as I finish it. Two, you repeat the song as soon as One finishes. Three, you repeat it after Two. Then, we'll start over again. Got it?"

"Yep."

"Okay, while we're at it, we're going to do a little dance. That will get our blood circulating and raise our body heat. Just follow the movements I do." with that explanation, Emily hopped up on her hind legs and started singing a silly song. The puppies laughed out loud and started following.

Fifty minutes later, laughing, singing, dancing and thoroughly distracted from the cold, wind and snow, they reached the exit to the forest and feasted their eyes on a giant black and white Akita and two cats rolling in the snow laughing their heads off.

Ten

Two days later, CB, Storm and Keiko stood in the warm sunshine of the farm talking to Emily. The storm had lasted another seven hours after the pups were saved. Keiko had made it home before her human, and was sleeping quietly in the thick snow when she got home, her thick double coat keeping her plenty warm.

Emily, CB and Storm had taken the pups to Emily's farm, where her humans had taken them in, fed them and called their humans to come pick them up.

Now, Emily finished her story for the third time, with the others pelting her with questions all the way.

"Look, you guys can ask me a thousand times, and my answer will always be the same. I have no idea if the big, fat guy in the red and white suit with the white beard was real. I was frozen, I am pretty sure I was close to dying, I obviously wasn't thinking clearly, and suddenly there he was.

"He was kind and helpful and he made me see that there was more inside myself than I ever believed possible. He also saved my life, and ultimately the pups lives, by pointing me toward the small cave." she said.

"But," Storm said, "where did he come from, and where did he go?"

"I don't know. He just appeared and then disappeared."

"So it could easily have just been your imagination?" CB said.

"Could have been, that's for sure. But, those footprints were real." she said emphatically.

"For sure, no doubts?" Keiko asked.

"Nope, no doubts. Definitely sure... the footprints were real, I definitely saw them."

"Well, that really is something, isn't it." CB said, "Whatever it was I just have to say I completely agree with him. There is a lot more to you than any of us thought. We owe you a gigantic debt of gratitude. And, a massive apology."

"Apology for what?"

"For not looking deeper into you when we met a few months ago, and not being more creative in helping you out. We were wrong, and for that we apologize." CB said.

"Thanks, but actually, it's me who needs to apologize. I really didn't give you any options, did I? I had a lot of growing up to do, and a lot of genetics to come to grips with. You helped me with that, and I really hope that what happened a couple days ago will be just the start of who I eventually will become."

"Well, whatever we can do to help, we're always there for you." Keiko said.

"Speaking of that, I've already had a chat with Ben. He said the he really has a need for a good tracker. Apparently, he is having trouble with squirrels, coyotes and a pesky badger. He could use someone with your skills." CB said.

"That would be fantastic, I'd love to help. Heck, I know all about that badger, I know just what to do with her." Emily laughed.

"Well, looks like we have a deal. Welcome to the team, Emily, we are ever so proud to have you."

Later that afternoon, CB and Storm sat next to Keiko in her yard pondering all that had happened over the past few days, and the strange man in the red suit.

"What is it about this time of year? I don't get it." Storm said.

"Well, I'm pretty sure that makes three of us. But, it is a special time, isn't it. Maybe you were right a few days ago. Maybe we should take some time each year to re-evaluate things a little. I think if Emily taught us anything this week, it's that no one is beyond hope." CB opined.

"That's a pretty good lesson for sure. We'll have to make sure we keep it in mind."

As the sun continued is slow descent, the three friends settled in for a quiet evening of chatting. Other projects would arise, but for now, old friends did what they enjoyed most... they spent quiet time with old friends.

Dear reader,

If you enjoyed these stories, please go to Amazon.com and write a quick review. The feedback is always appreciated, and it helps other readers make their purchase decisions.

For other stories you might enjoy, check out the rest of my books by searching for Wm. Dudley on amazon.com.

Thank you very much for your support, it is greatly appreciated.

Wm. Dudley

Made in United States
Orlando, FL
22 December 2023

41596421R00138